With
Fondest
Regards

ALSO BY FRANÇOISE SAGAN:

Bonjour Tristesse
A Certain Smile
Those Without Shadows
Aimez-Vous Brahms?
The Wonderful Clouds
La Chamade
The Heartkeeper
A Few Hours of Sunlight
Scars on the Soul
Lost Profile
Silken Eyes (Stories)
The Unmade Bed
The Painted Lady
Incidental Music (Stories)
Salad Days

With Fondest Regards
FRANÇOISE SAGAN

Translated by Christine Donougher

E. P. DUTTON · NEW YORK

Originally published in France under the title
AVEC MON MEILLEUR SOUVENIR by Gallimard
Copyright © Editions Gallimard, 1984

This English translation copyright © 1985 by W. H. Allen & Co. PLC.

The poem on page 169 is reprinted by permission of New Directions
from *Illuminations and Other Prose Poems* by Arthur Rimbaud,
translated by Louise Varèse. © 1957 by New Directions.

Published in the United States by
E. P. Dutton, 2 Park Avenue, New York, N.Y. 10016

Library of Congress Cataloging in Publication Data
Sagan, Françoise, 1935–
With fondest regards.
Translation of: Avec mon meilleur souvenir.
1. Sagan, Françoise, 1935–   —Biography.
2. Authors, French—20th century—Biography.   I. Title.
PQ2633.U74Z46213   1985   843'.914 [B]   85-1489
ISBN 0-525-24334-8

Published simultaneously in Canada
by Fitzhenry & Whiteside Limited, Toronto

Designed by Mark O'Connor

COBE

10 9 8 7 6 5 4 3 2 1

First Edition

To my mother

I would have shown the children
the gilt-head bream of the blue deep,
those fish of gold, those fish that sing.

—RIMBAUD, *Le Bateau Ivre*

Contents

Billie Holiday

New York is a wide open, streamlined city, breezy and bracing, with two sparkling rivers: the Hudson and the East River. Day and night, it pulses with strong-smelling sea winds, winds full of salt and car fumes by day, of spilled alcohol by night. New York smells of ozone, fresh tar and the sea. New York is a tall young blonde woman, showy and provocative in the sunshine, as beautiful as Baudelaire's "dream of stone." And like some tall women too blonde to be true, New York has its dark and somber places, private, hidden, despoiled. In short, if the reader will forgive me a commonplace (and what choice have you?), New York is an enthralling city.

And enthralled I was, instantly, the first time I went there, although I had been invited by my publisher and suffered the drawbacks of such an invitation: the cares and constraints of an author on tour. No sooner had I returned to Paris than I began to dream of going back a free agent; which is what I did a year or two later, free of all encumbrances—even those of solitude, since I went with my good friend Michel Magne, a composer who has since made his name in film music and experiments with synthesizers. Michel Magne could not speak a word of English, but his wit knew no bounds, and he managed, with a minimum of expletives, to put up with the passersby who threw banana skins and cigarette butts into the same box into which he posted his love letters—a box whose purpose, as far as he could see, was clearly indicated by the words "Litter Drop." Anyway, he shared my obsession of ten years' standing (I must have been twenty-two or -three at the time): to meet and hear, live, Billie Holiday, the Diva of Jazz, the First Lady of Jazz, Lady Day, the Callas, the Star, the Voice of Jazz. For Michel Magne and myself, she was the Voice of America; not yet—to us anyway—the heartrending, strangled voice of black America, but rather the voluptuous, gravelly,

4

playful voice of jazz in its purest form. From "Stormy Weather" to "Strange Fruit," from "Body and Soul" to "Solitude," Jack Teagarden to Barney Bigard, Roy Eldridge to Barney Kessel—Michel Magne and I had, independently but at the same age, wept openly or exulted as we listened to her sing.

Hardly had we arrived at the Pierre—the only hotel I knew, since it was there my status-conscious publisher had installed me on my first visit—than we asked, then begged, then demanded to know where we could hear Billie Holiday sing. We imagined her, as usual, taking Carnegie Hall by storm. After much sanctimonious hemming and hawing we were given the following information—today the same story would make any concert hall director in the world double up with laughter: that Billie Holiday had recently taken certain narcotics on stage and was now banned from performing in New York for several months!

In 1956 America was still very puritanical. And, on reflection, rather vindictive—since it took us three days to find out that Billie Holiday was singing in a club in Connecticut. "In Connecticut? No problem. Taxi! Take us to Connecticut!"

Connecticut was not the New York suburb we imagined it to be, and we drove nearly two hundred miles in freezing cold weather before reaching a wild, colorful place that seemed to me far from anywhere—a kind of country-music club with an uninspired-looking clientele that was noisy, rowdy and restless. Suddenly we saw a tall stout black woman with exceptionally large eyes emerge from the crowd. She closed her eyes for a moment before starting to sing, and immediately we were transported into other galaxies: cheerful, desperate, sensual or cynical, as she wanted.

We were in ecstasy. It was beyond our wildest dreams. And I believe we would have made the icy, two-hundred-mile return trip in the same state of ecstasy even if someone had not suddenly taken it upon himself to introduce us to her. Here were these two intrepid French visitors it was explained, who had crossed the vast expanse of the Atlantic, the suburbs of New York, and the boundaries of Connecticut just to hear her sing. "Oh, dears," she said softly. "How crazy you are!"

Two days later we tracked her down again at Eddie Condon's at four in the morning—as far as she was concerned the only reasonable hour of day and the most convenient for everyone. Eddie Condon was, I think, the owner of a nightclub very much in vogue at the time—a nightclub for whites, located downtown—and he loved jazz enough that, once the last drinker had left, he would turn his club over to musicians with a thirst for something else. At 3:30 A.M. he closed the main door; we entered via a service entrance into the huge nightclub that was practically pitch-black. Only the white tablecloths, already laid out for the following day, stood out against the darkness, and only the piano, a double bass and the brass trumpets gleamed under the spotlights on stage.

For two weeks we spent our nights (or rather our dawns, from 4 A.M. to midday) in that perpetually smoky club, listening to Billie Holiday sing. Michel would accompany her sometimes on the piano, an honor he was madly proud of; and when it wasn't Michel playing, it was another of the countless musicians in attendance, another of Billie Holiday's adoring fans who had picked up the news of her whereabouts relayed through the night by drums on the New York jazz circuit. One after another, from one club or another, they all made their way here, to join us at daybreak. The audience consisted only of the two of us from France, two or three friends of Lady Day herself and her husband, her man of the moment, a big morose fellow with whom she would have violent exchanges. On stage, there were, besides Cozy Cole on drums, twenty well-known jazzmen, each more famous than the next. Gerry Mulligan would duo along with the voice of our friend (she was a friend by then) against a background of flowing alcohol, exploding laughter, misunderstandings and occasional angry scenes that blew up as quickly as they blew over. Our friend Billie Holiday—who would pat us on the head like children, and who was separated from us (though we ourselves had not the slightest intimation of it) by a tragic past and a terrifying destiny, a stormy and violent life, but one so talented that just by closing her eyes and allowing a sort of moan to well up in her throat—amused, cynical and profoundly vulnerable—she could satisfy her desires and blot out her sorrows. It was the inimitable cry of a conquering and despotic personality, regal in her complete naturalness; for there was nothing affected about her, nothing that seemed contrived.

I did not realize then that such vitality eclipses all the labyrinthine complexities of even the most introspective and perverse minds. I did not realize how she bared herself to experience, raw and almost bleeding, how she plunged into life, amid blows and caresses that she seemed to defy simply by breathing. She was a *femme fatale* in the sense that *fate* had seized her from the very beginning and had never let her go. And the only defense that fate had allowed her, after a thousand sorrows and a thousand equally violent joys, was that humorous inflection of her voice, that bizarrely raucous note when she had gone far, far away, or deep down in the depths, and suddenly returned to us, obliquely, via her little bantering laugh and her proud but fearful eyes.

We slept very little during those days, and I

could swear that at times we walked straight up
the middle of Fifth Avenue in the sunshine, just
myself, her, and Michel, alone in an empty town.
A town where, after the blast of the saxophones
and the flourishes on the drums and the brilliant
explosion of her voice, now, by a strange process
of saturation, there was only the echo of our footsteps on the pavement. I could swear that I saw
New York at midday totally deserted except for this
great lady and her taciturn companion who, having quickly hugged us, would disappear into one
of those long black, dusty limousines straight out
of a B-movie. I am at a loss to say what else we
did during the day. Apart from a few hours when
we could not help but go to sleep, it seemed to
me that we wandered about like zombies in a town
that was deaf and dumb, in which the only point
of vitality and only refuge was that stage, the dim
spotlights, the broken-backed piano, and this
woman who sometimes said she had drunk too
much to sing and then would play around with the
words of her songs, mixing them up and finding
alternatives, some funny, some heartrending, none
of which I can remember. Strange to say, this for-
getfulness has never caused me any regrets. New
York had become such a dark and cheerless
place—apart from the brilliance of her voice—that
we let ourselves be lulled by it, let our weariness
and our recklessness, our drunkenness, be lulled

in this warm night with the rhythms of the sea. A sea in which no precise memory could remain on the surface without seeming trivial, just a piece of wreckage.

It was on a night just as dark that I met up with her again a year or two later in Paris. I must have written to her once or twice to thank her, and to ask how she was getting on, but she had not replied—she was not the kind of person who writes letters—so it was through the newspaper that I found out that she was going to sing one evening at the Mars Club, in the Impasse Marbeuf. I had lost contact with Michel Magne, and it was my husband who accompanied me that night. We arrived well before she did, at the dark little nightclub, a thousand leagues and more removed from Eddie Condon's gigantic place, more intimate and more intimidating, too, because that night there was a real audience, if a limited one. Toward midnight, as I was beginning to get impatient, someone pushed open the door and came in, followed by a noisy group of people.

It was Billie Holiday—and yet it wasn't. She had grown thin; she had aged; and her arms bore the ever closer tracks of needles. She no longer had that innate assurance, that physical equilibrium which had conferred on her such marble-like serenity amid the storms and dizzy turbulence of her life.

We fell into each other's arms. She began to laugh and I instantly recovered a sense of exaltation, that romantic childlike exultation I had known in a now-distant New York, a New York clothed in music and the night as some children are clothed only in blue or white. I introduced my husband to her; he was rather disconcerted by her presence, which seemed both completely natural and at the same time quite exotic; and it was only then that I realized how many million light-years of difference there were between us, or rather, how many million years of darkness separated me from her, and how she had so wonderfully and with such friendliness been happy to wipe out that difference during the fortnight now long past. A host of things had been put aside during our first meeting: the problem of race, of her courage, of her fight to the death against poverty, prejudice, lack of identity, against whites and non-whites; against alcohol, the wickedness of enemies, against Harlem, against New York; against the passions provoked by the color of a person's skin, and the almost equally violent passions that can be provoked by talent and success. She had never allowed us to think of any of those things, neither Michel nor myself, though we might well have thought of them for ourselves. We "sensitive" Europeans had been the uncaring barbarians on that occasion. This idea brought tears to my eyes, and the rest of that evening would not find them dry.

Billie Holiday was no longer accompanied by her husband but by two or three young people, Swedes or Americans, I don't remember now, who fussed about her, but, it seemed to me, were as alien to her fate as I was myself. Full of admiration for her, but hopelessly ineffectual, they had organized nothing for the evening and there was not even, fantastically enough, anything resembling a microphone on the black piano she was already resting against, apparently unaware of the applause. It was a fiasco. People were on all fours trying to fix up an old mike that crackled terribly; someone ran off to La Villa d'Este or somewhere else to find another. Everyone became bad-tempered and worked up, to no avail, and after a while, as if resigned to the chaos, she came and sat down at our table.

She drank distractedly and spoke to me occasionally, her voice husky, smoke-roughened and sarcastic; she remained indifferent to what was going on around us, though she was the center of it all. She said very little to my friends, except to ask my first husband whether he beat me, something—she declared ironically, and to my own detriment—that he ought to do. My protests made her laugh, and for a moment I recognized the echo of her laughter at Eddie Condon's; a time when we were all, it seemed, young and happy and gifted; a time when the microphone worked or rather— though I hardly dared admit it to myself—a time when she didn't need a microphone to sing. In the end she sang a few songs—with or without a microphone, I don't remember any more—accompanied rather hesitantly by a quartet that tried to follow the unpredictable vagaries of her voice, which itself had become a little uncertain. My admiration was such—or was it the force of memory?—that I could not help but admire her, despite the awful, ridiculous shortcomings of this meager recital. She sang with eyes lowered. She would skip a verse and have difficulty catching her breath. She clung to the piano as if to a ship's rail in stormy seas. No doubt the rest of the audience had come in the same spirit as I had, for they applauded wildly, and she looked on them with a pity and irony that were in fact a harsh judgment upon herself.

After those few snatches of song, she came and sat with us for a moment. She was in a hurry, a terrible hurry, because she was leaving the next day, I think, for London, or somewhere else in Europe, she couldn't remember where exactly. "Anyway, darling," she said to me in English, "you know I am going to die very soon in New York, between two cops." Of course I swore she was wrong. I could not and did not want to believe her; all my adolescence, those years that were lulled and entranced by her voice, refused to believe her. So my first reaction was total amazement when I opened a newspaper a few months later, and read that Billie Holiday had died the night before, alone in a hospital, between two cops.

Games of
Chance

I first became acquainted with gambling one June 21st. Born on the first day of summer, I approached the gaming tables with firm resolve on the evening of my twenty-first birthday. I entered the Palm Beach in Cannes with a godfather on either side of me, both of whom were amused to witness my debut on the green baize. They did indeed witness the start of my career, but they were not there to see where it led, for by then I had escaped their surveillance and was racing from casino to casino without them.

(N.B. Contrary to what's been said about me, it's not true that I have lost any "fortunes" on the green baize, never having had one—strangely enough—at my disposal. I have lost at the tables only what my way of life has left me to play with, a life not of luxury but of dreaming—a dream that meant I should have no material cares and that the only cause for worry and anguish in the faces of those around me should be the pain of love. The kind of protection with which I've always sought to safeguard my immediate present, heedless of days to come, has never left me the smallest fortune to squander in games of chance. And so I've had no difficulty in always playing beyond my means, which is the very essence of gambling. Moreover, I tend to win when I gamble, odd as it may seem, and the owners of the casinos where I've played must laugh bitterly whenever anyone refers to the millions that I'm supposed to have lost at their tables. I wanted to make this parenthetical aside in the event I should be suspected of masochism, and so that gambling not be seen as some evil companion of mine. Just as my friends have been good friends to me, so too has chance been a good companion, changeable certainly, but both ways.)

So my first encounter took place with some ceremony. In those days in Cannes at the end of June,

some of the most famous patrons of the Palm
Beach would come face to face. Darryl Zanuck was
there, as were, I think, the Cognac-Hennessys, and
Jack Warner, and other giants among the great
gamblers of all time. Wisely, I was kept away from
this table and, more bewildered than impressed,
merely observed the conflict among Titans. I
learned the rules of chemin de fer, learned that
on a single hand of just two cards with a combined value of eight or nine one stood to win fifty
million old francs—although one then had to stake
those winnings double or quits on the next hand,
again of just two cards. More than the enormity of
the sums involved, it was the speed with which they
changed hands that fascinated me. I fancied myself gambling with my destiny, just like that, in two
quick hands. I did not realize that in the casino as
much as anywhere else, wealth takes the form of
checks, that these checks are accepted with greater
or lesser willingness by the casinos concerned, and
that the often mean-spirited prudence of the
managers of gaming clubs acts as a brake, sometimes salutary, sometimes fatal, on the mania of
players.

I ended up with my guardian angels, or rather
my demon spirits, at a little roulette table, where
I was amazed to discover that my favorite numbers were three, eight, and eleven—a fact of which
I had been totally unaware and which turned out
to be unalterable. I discovered that I preferred

black to red, odd numbers to even, low to high, and other instinctive choices that would no doubt be of great interest to psychoanalysts. I lost a little, then won betting on a single number. This seemed perfectly natural to me, but struck my companions as quite amazing. "Imagine that! After only five minutes, a single number!" I went and lost my winnings on a game of chemin de fer: I was having trouble making sense of the value of the cards, so I was partnered with a charming croupier who decided how I should play. In this way, I discovered that when the odds were even I would not draw at five. (Any player who reads this will now have a complete profile of my style of play.)

And something else I discovered for myself was that, at the gaming table more than anywhere else, it was important to conceal one's emotions. In the course of a single evening I had seen it all, betrayed on people's faces with the kind of intensity and exaggeration affected by certain ham actors: distrust, credulity, disappointment, anger, passion, stubbornness, exasperation, relief, exultation and, even more unconvincingly, indifference. And so I decided that, come what may, whatever the blessings or blows of fate, I would meet them always with smiles and graciousness. And just as my favorite numbers have not changed, so neither has my attitude. I have even been congratulated on my sangfroid by one or two super-phlegmatic Englishmen, and I confess I take more pride in this than in the few other virtues I may have—or thought I had—displayed in my life.

I will not seek to explain here the appeal of gambling; either you are susceptible to it, or you aren't. You are born a gambler just as you are born with red hair, or intelligence, or a malicious nature. The non-gambler should skip the next few pages and anecdotes which will delight or appall only my co-religionists. It is true that gambling is a profoundly absorbing pastime. It is true that you can keep the person you love most waiting for two hours if you are involved in a game that affords any relish. It is true that you can almost completely forget your debts, and the constraints and restrictions that bind you, in pursuit of the croupier's shoe, only to come to an hour later and find your problems have increased tenfold. But what an hour! Your heart races, you lose all notion of time, forget the value of money, forget the tentacle-like shackles of society. It is true that as you play, money becomes once more what it should never cease to be, a game, chips, something that must be traded for something else and that in itself is meaningless. It is also true that real gamblers are rarely wicked, miserly or aggressive. They have a toleration for others shared by all those who are not afraid to lose what they have; those who consider that all material possessions and moral tenets have no lasting value. For them every setback is no more than a stroke of bad luck, and every victory a gift from heaven.

The truth of this is even more evident on the racetrack than in the casino, where the fast pace of events leads to a frenzy that is sometimes disagreeable. Generally speaking, except on the days when the Grand Prix is being run at Longchamps, you'll find no trace of the prejudices that poison the lives of so-called democratic peoples on the turf where the toteboard rules. There are no social distinctions, no rich and no poor. There are only winners and losers, and the size of their winnings or losses is irrelevant. I have seen a group of stevedores consoling Guy de Rothschild with unquestionable sincerity when his horse did not come in. I have seen wealthy Parisian women beg the barman for a racing tip, and notorious layabouts become the object of general admiration as they wave their ten-franc ticket in triumph. More than their moral failing, their fanaticism and their fatal obsession, one should remember that gamblers are above all like children. Even if it is indeed the food from their cherished infant's mouth that they are staking on a rank outsider, what they see at stake is their reputation: to win all afternoon at Auteuil or Vincennes, to have your hunches proved right seven races in a row, endows you with the status of a star, a glory that few men, or indeed women worthy of the name, can easily resist. And conversely, to lose consistently for as many days on end, to have not a single horse come in, can turn you into a pariah, one of the damned, as wretched as those believers in the Middle Ages when they thought they had fallen from grace and that God had ceased to love them.

But let's get back to gambling, real gambling; that is to say, the kind of gambling that can carry you further than you might think, the kind of gambling that is of course a great deal less of a hazard on the racetrack than at the casino. The betting offices at the Parimutuel do not give credit and don't accept checks, so many unlucky punters drop out after the third or fourth race. They might not be very happy about it, but they have no choice. At the casino, on the other hand, as long as you have a little credit to your name, it's a much more serious business.

At the age of twenty-one, I was thought to be a multi-millionaire, and several gaming managers still basked in this heady conviction. I was soon back again, three months after my debut at Cannes, at the Casino in Monte Carlo, involved in an epic game, with King Farouk himself sitting next to me. I still did not know how to figure out the value of the cards, and the following two incidents occurred: I passed with a hand worth one point which I had mistaken for a seven; Farouk, with a four, drew a six, which of course meant that I had won; but when I laid my hand down, a wave of amazement and indignation ran round the table. Since it was after all my unquestionable privilege to lose, I was given the shoe, and this time in my panic I took a card, with a seven in my hand, and drew a Queen, which beat Farouk's six. He was close to apoplexy, and some of the women let fall their diamonds because of it. So it was decided that I should play with a croupier to advise me. I certainly won that evening, but I don't remember ever having been so embarrassed to have done so.

The season closed without further incident—Saint-Tropez, thank God, did not have a casino, and it was only later, when Saint-Tropez was overrun and became impossible in the summer, that I beat a retreat to the more tranquil beaches of Normandy. I rented a big, dusty, dilapidated house above Honfleur, and I was all ready to spend the month of July swimming in the sea when I discovered two situations that, alas, went hand in hand: the sea was always miles out, but the casino at Deauville was always open. Instead of days spent in the sunshine, there were nights without sleep. For Bernard Frank, Jacques Chazot and me, there was only the dawn and the night, with sometimes a glimpse of grass in between. The singing of birds was drowned by the click of chips, green baize took the place of green fields.

On August 7, the day before I was supposed to vacate the house, which meant checking an inventory that promised to be troublesome, we went for what we thought was the last time to the large white casino, which then still belonged to André. Soon ruined at a game of chemin de fer, I withdrew to the roulette table where by dawn, thanks to the eight which came up immediately and continued to do so, I was in possession of eighty thousand new francs (this in 1960).

We returned to the house in excellent spirits, only to find the owner himself at the front door with the inventory under his arm. He pointed out rather severely that it was eight o'clock in the morning, the time we had agreed to vacate. I was about to start going through the dreaded inventory with him when, out of the blue, he asked me whether I wanted to buy the house. I opened my mouth to say that I was a born tenant, that I never bought anything, when he added: "Considering the work that needs doing, I won't ask much, I'll let you have it for 80,000 francs." It was August 8, I had won on the eight, he was selling it for eight million old francs, it was eight o'clock in the morning—what else could I do in the circumstances? I drew the banknotes out of my bulging evening bag and went to bed in triumph in what was to be—and has remained to this day—the only property on earth I own: a house that is still rather dilapidated, situated two miles from Honfleur and seven from Deauville.

Let no one come tell me of the evils of gambling or the misfortune that weighs on gamblers. I shall say nothing of the endless repairs or the various disasters that ownership of this country house has entailed—and with which any property owner will be familiar. Instead I shall cite the twenty-five wonderful years during which I faithfully returned to the house, twenty-five years of sunshine and rain and rhododendrons and the happy holidays I have spent there. Mortgaged twenty times over, nearly sold on two occasions, a workplace for my working friends and a refuge for lovers, this house is today worth eight billion memories.

And of course the same house has witnessed countless dawn returns, in triumph or despair, but always in that spirit of excitement and insouciance which accompanies the practice of gambling. Thousands of anecdotes surface in my memory, just thinking of those breakfasts drinking coffee or champagne, when doors were carefully closed without a sound if we had lost, or burst open on any unfortunate sleeper with cries of triumph: "We're celebrating!" There was the time someone made sixty thousand francs, having started with only two hundred; and the time when, because I didn't speak clearly, my last hundred francs were placed on the thirty and not on low by a harassed croupier, and the thirty won. There was the time when a friend won back twice over everything his girlfriend had lost, and the time when another friend won enough to buy the car of his girlfriend's dreams. There was the time we all had to chip in to pay for the gas to drive back to Paris, not to mention the innumerable occasions when we had to borrow money from the doorman to pay for the taxi home.

Strangely enough, memories of winning are always more vivid. You only remember the good times, just as you only remember congenial players. You cannot imagine the number of friends and acquaintances you can make in twenty-five years of gambling, and yet never know their names. You see the same faces night after night, for three months, then sometimes again the following year, then sometimes for three years in a row. You do not talk to one another except to say hello; smiles of congratulation or regret are exchanged, depending on how the other is faring. You share your fortune good and bad, bound by ties closer than any that the most intimate confidences might create. There are friends like these that you do not lose (and there are a few whose death you learn of, by chance, from a valet, and you are absurdly upset, much more so than you would have thought possible). You also come across gamblers who play too hard, whom you see at the beginning of August showing off in flashy cars, and who appear at the Bar du Soleil looking more haggard every day, and at the end of a fortnight you learn of their urgent departure. "*Adieu* calves, cows, pigs, hens . . . *adieu* to those dawns beneath the domed casino. *Adieu* to the whiteness of the sea and the empty beaches, *adieu* to the galloping of the first horses prancing in the light that you flee, your eyes stinging with cigarette smoke . . ."

It was after a run of bad luck that I decided one fine evening, one tragic evening of Dostoevskian complexion, to have myself barred from Deauville for the next five years. Let me say straight away that those years were a nightmare. No amount of trumpet-playing on any number of records was able to drown the subtle sound of chips clicking over our heads, and whenever I heard the croupier's deep voice saying "*Rien ne va plus,* no more bets" as we passed by the entrance to the Casino on our way to go dancing, his voice seemed to resound like that of Moses, like that of a beneficent but stern God who had cast us out from the security of his flock. I say "we" because my true and loyal friends shared my misery and exile, and slipped away one after the other only with the greatest discretion to return to the green pastures of forbidden pleasures. Denying oneself anything at all ought not to be allowed; at least that was the thought that came to haunt me—too late, alas. Since I hated Monte Carlo, where I went only rarely to play, there was nothing for it but to go to London.

There was no reason for me to go to London, but my literary agent drew my attention to a sinister individual there, whose name and occupation I have completely forgotten, who was amassing a fortune at my expense. He owed me the sum of twenty-five thousand francs, I believe, and refused to send it to me. I decided to set off with my agent on a mission to recover the money, partly because my finances were not in very good shape, and partly because I didn't know London very well—in fact even now I hardly know it—and I remembered that I had a charming friend there whom I had not seen for a long time. This was ten years ago, and the cost of the tickets and hotel would still leave me with reasonable funds. So we set off, and stayed in a hotel that brought to mind Agatha Christie.

On the very first evening, with my agent in tow, I had dinner with my charming friend. We dined at Annabel's—at that time, *the* place to go—and when we reached the dessert, my English friend pointed out that directly overhead, on the second floor, was the Clermont Club. I had heard several friends describe it, in tones of horror and delight combined, as a typically English club, where the temperature of the game was high though the players would display all the coolness for which the British are renowned. So we went upstairs. I was introduced by my friend, and knowing me all too well, he then left me alone for an hour at the chemin de fer table and went back downstairs to drink my health with my agent, who was already suffering some misgivings.

I surveyed the scene around me. It was a large, comfortable, wood-paneled room, with leather furniture and a few inimitable specimens of English society: racehorse owners who, between each banco, talked only of the turf; two outrageous old ladies with flowery hats and enormous jewels; a degenerate young heir who bore the name of one of the best English families; and opposite me sat a socialite friend from Paris who rolled his eyes in horror when he saw me sit down at that awesome table. The stakes were all in guineas and I had no idea of their value. Someone muttered an inaudible explanation in my ear, the manager arranged for a little pile of chips to be brought to me in exchange for a little piece of paper which I happily signed, and play began.

It was very pleasant, I must admit. The English are the best gamblers in the world, as everyone knows, and gambling really seems to raise their spirits. To my left there was talk of horses, to my right it was regattas, and opposite, foreign travel was the topic of conversation. Meanwhile, my little pile of chips disappeared one after the other, to a general lack of concern, including my own. Hardly had one little pile disappeared than a haughty valet would place another on a silver tray in front of me. I would sign his little piece of paper, and so it continued. I was awakened from this happy state of lethargy an hour later by the sudden appearance of my agent's face looming over me. He looked quite green. He too mumbled something incomprehensible, in which the words ''ruined,'' ''disaster'' and the like recurred. That was when I noticed that my Parisian friend opposite had turned quite red, and far from rolling his eyes as he had done at the start of the game, he was now staring at me with a peculiar expression on his face, like that of a wounded she-wolf, I thought to myself.

Feeling slightly alarmed, I discreetly asked the alacritous valet to write down on a little piece of paper the sum I now owed. He went over to speak to a tall, well-built man, who was very nice, and had been circling our table since play began. He was none other than the owner of the Clermont Club. He did a quick calculation, wrote a figure on a piece of paper and the trusty messenger brought it over to me with the same alacrity he had previously demonstrated. I glanced at it. I had to draw on all my moral precepts, all my strength of mind, all the good upbringing my parents had tried to give me and all the bad that I had succeeded in acquiring by myself, not to fall over backwards. My debt totaled eighty thousand pounds—its value would be twice that today—and I had nowhere near even a quarter of it in my bank account.

"*C'est à vous,*" the genial person sitting next to me said in an atrocious accent as he pushed the shoe towards me. With what I hoped was a steady hand, I pushed half of my remaining chips on a nine; they instantly disappeared. So I passed on the shoe and tried to think. To pay off my debt, I would have to give up the flat where I was living, ask my mother to take care of my son, find a one-room apartment nearby and for the next two years work exclusively for the benefit of the taxman and

the Clermont Club. I could say goodbye to holidays, car, outings, clothes and a carefree existence. It was a catastrophe.

So catastrophic, I thought, that if I was going
to lose two years of my life anyway, losing four
would make no difference. I raised my hand rather
idly and the alacritous valet was immediately at my
side with the wretched little stack on his wretched
tray. Once more I signed one of his wretched little chits and in a ringing voice asked to play banco
next time round. I won. After that I played banco
whenever I had the opportunity. I was gambling
recklessly, as though there were no tomorrow, as
they say, and—what a miracle!—it was all coming
back again. I watched my little pile become a big
pile at a rate that was unbearably slow and at the
same time prodigiously fast. From time to time, I
would ask the footman to relieve me of all these
things that were getting in my way, and he would
return one of my little notes, having torn it in half.
After an hour had passed in this wanton way, I
discreetly enquired of the silk-stockinged messenger how I now stood with the house. He went
and spoke to the proprietor who, it seemed to me
from what I could see out of the corner of my eye,
was much quicker in his calculation, the result of
which was brought back to me on another little
note, which I unfolded without betraying any haste.
I now owed only fifty pounds. All this time, I might

---

add, I had had to discuss the Epsom Derby with the person on my left, and the attractions of Florida with the person on my right.

I stood up, suddenly weary, and cordially took my leave of everyone at the table, who responded just as cordially. I went to pay my fifty pounds to the cashier. The proprietor saw me out, accompanying me as far as the staircase descending to Annabel's—the same staircase I had climbed two hours earlier feeling very lighthearted, and down which I had almost returned a pauper an hour later.

"It was a great pleasure to have you play at my tables," said this very friendly man, "especially since the French are generally so lacking in sangfroid when gambling."

"Oh," I said, in a voice that seemed thin even to me, "oh, the very idea. One plays for the fun of it, don't you agree?"

And I went down the steps tottering slightly on my high heels. My English friend found the story highly amusing, but my agent was dead drunk and we had the greatest difficulty getting him back to the hotel. When I attended a fashionable dinner party in Paris a week later, I realized that the tale of my London adventure had already been told by the Parisian who had witnessed the event, for I was treated with the kind of esteem and superstitious awe normally reserved for someone who has survived an airplane disaster.

This anecdote has no other purpose or concern except to illustrate more clearly the danger of any kind of prohibition—even if self-imposed. And that is why a week before my period of abstinence was to end, I wrote to the Prefect of Police to inform a no doubt totally indifferent official that I was about to revert to my former frivolous behavior. Deauville had after all proved less dangerous than London, and the franc less treacherous than the guinea. (Even though I had made a long-shot recovery.)

This is why, I believe, you meet so many gamblers outside casinos in a state of great hilarity although they have not won a thing. "I lost two hundred francs!" they say with glee, to the great astonishment of non-players. What it means simply is that there was a time in the course of the evening when they had lost a great deal more. Which also explains why people always talk of the masochism of gamblers. Gamblers do not like losing—real gamblers, I mean. But sometimes they consider themselves lucky to lose less at the end of a game than they were losing while it was in progress. They regard this as an achievement and are proud of themselves—quite rightly so, for make no mistake: gambling requires not only madness, recklessness and the presence in your psychological makeup of a terrible and discreditable moral failing, but also a steady nerve, will power, and virtue in the Latin sense of the word *virtus*, meaning courage. When you have been losing all afternoon, have gone a whole week without a break, when you feel as though you have been abandoned by the gods, by luck, and even by yourself, and suddenly the game starts to go in your favor, it takes a supreme effort to force yourself to believe in it, to seize fortune by the forelock, cling to it and take advantage of it.

Very recently I was on a losing streak for ten days, playing for not very large stakes at a casino in the Manche, and every day the hope of recovering my losses and the total impossibility of paying off my debt brought me back to the tables. On the twelfth day I suddenly struck lucky, on two tables. I plunged in and bet non-stop on numbers and colors, on low and on groups of numbers. Once again, it took me an hour to recover my losses (and, in fact, my numbers only came up for an hour). I left the casino accompanied by the half-horrified, half-admiring glances of the croupiers, having lost no more than three hundred francs and bursting with pride and joy. I am prepared to admit that even at the occasionally successful open-

ings of my plays, or while reading certain sometimes ecstatic reviews of my books, I have rarely
known, in fact I have never known, such an over-
whelming sense of pride. Despite the cold, I drove
home that evening in an old car with the roof
down, accompanied by a group of exultant friends,
and the return journey along the coast road from
Deauville to Honfleur was one of the most delightful experiences of my life. I had spent a week
in purgatory, and it had almost ended in disaster.
But I had successfully extricated myself. The sea
on my left was gray, the grass to my right was dark
green, and the whole world was mine. After ten
days' exertion and nervous tension, I had managed to lose just three hundred francs. I couldn't
have been happier.

This conclusion may seem ridiculous, I know,
but once again, this piece on gambling was in-
tended only for the eyes of gamblers.

Tennessee Williams

In 1953 I wrote *Bonjour Tristesse*, which was published in France in 1954 and enjoyed a *succès de scandale*. I could not understand what all the fuss was about at first, and today I can think of only two ridiculous reasons for it. It was inconceivable that a young girl of seventeen or eighteen should make love, without being in love, with a boy of her own age, and not be punished for it. People couldn't tolerate the idea that the girl should not fall madly in love with the boy, and not be pregnant by the end of the summer. It was unacceptable too in those days that a young girl should have the right to use her body as she will, and derive pleasure from it without incurring a penalty, one which had always been thought inevitable. And furthermore, people couldn't accept that this same young girl should know about her father's love affairs, discuss them with him, and thereby reach a kind of complicity with him on subjects that had until then been taboo between parents and children.

The rest of the book was, I'm sure, totally innocuous, certainly when I consider what things are like today, thirty years later. In a laughable and almost cruel reversal, it has become indecent, even ridiculous, not to make love as soon as one is old enough; and parents and children are now set irrevocably apart by a complicity that the experience of both tells them is quite false but which they cannot help but affect (with parents resenting their children for being young and children resenting their parents for being no longer young yet wanting to behave as if they were).

Of course an era during which, to begin with, parents alone had the right to judge the behavior of children, as if the children were a helot class, cannot be called a happy one; a time when children themselves had not even the glimmer of an idea—nor were they entitled to any—about the nature of their parents' private lives. Nevertheless, between a forty- and a twenty-year-old, there was a real difference of generation, one that by dint of obstinate determination has been destroyed, and its absence has come to be regarded as a monstrous obscenity by young and old alike.

For that reason, I think that if *Bonjour Tristesse* were published today it would now seem to portray a dream of innocence, a wonderful dream of what family relationships, and the sexual relationships of young people and their elders, might be like. In any case, today there would be no scandal. Yet it did cause a scandal in France and raised almost equally noisy protests in America.

I was nineteen. I did what I was told; and I was told I should go to America so that the Americans could see for themselves "the charming little monster" François Mauriac had described. Since he had written about me in those terms I had acquired a strange, almost mythic status, attracting admiration or scorn, rejection or acceptance. To cut a long story short, I was put aboard a Constellation, one of those big airplanes that hovered in the night at that time, and took, I think, twelve hours to fly the Atlantic. I had been persuaded to go to America to prove to them that the author of *Bonjour Tristesse* was not a little old lady with gray hair, that I wasn't some long-suffering individual collaborating with Editions Julliard in a cunning hoax. So off I went. I was still happy to comply with what I was told was necessary—I still believed in the idea of necessity—and besides, I was not wrong. Publicity *is* necessary if a book is to sell. But there are different categories of necessity in life, and that I did not know at the time.

My arrival in the United States took place in real *Dolce Vita* style, with dozens of photographers waiting for me at Kennedy Airport—it was called Idlewild then. It was dawn. I was very nearly twenty. There was a crowd waiting—in fact, for the next month, there would always be a crowd around me. My days were scheduled to the last minute, as if I were some obliging convict, and since my English was no better than at the time I took my *baccalauréat* (when I got a seven or eight out of twenty), my conversation was, to say the least, anodyne and noncommittal. It was two weeks before anyone noticed that I was signing copies of my books "with all my sympathies," imagining the line not an expression of condolence but of geniality, as in "*avec toute ma sympathie*"—which is how I signed books for French readers.

I was asked the same questions at least fifty times: about love, young girls and sexuality, subjects that were novel at the time, but already tedious. I was also treated to cocktail parties, lunches, dinners, even balls. And then one fine day, when I felt I couldn't take any more, I received out of the blue a telegram from Tennessee Williams, writer, poet and playwright. In the course of those endless interviews I had had occasion to say a hundred times that he was for me one of the most outstanding American writers. His telegram was an invitation to visit him at home, in Key West, Florida.

Immediately I backed out of a lunch at the consulate, some TV appearances scheduled for Channel 183, and a meeting with the editor of *Fishing Review* or God knows what. I fled from my hotel, raced to the airport and flew to Miami. In Miami three of us—my sister, a friend and I—rented a car. With memories of *Key Largo* and other crime thrillers in mind, we drove across Florida, with its swamps and marshes, over the bridges that connect one island to another, and arrived in the small garrison town of Key West. We went to a modest, rather gray-looking hotel called The Key Wester, where three rooms had been booked for us. We checked in, feeling slightly bemused, not really knowing what we were doing there, but already staggering beneath the terrific heat of a tropical sun.

At 6:30 we were told Tennessee Williams had arrived. A short man with blond hair and a gleam of amusement in his blue eyes made his appearance. Since the death of Whitman, he had been for me—and still remains—America's greatest poet. He was followed by a cheerful-looking, dark-haired man, perhaps the most charming man in America and Europe put together, whose name was Franco. He was a complete unknown and never became anything else. Behind them came a tall thin woman wearing shorts; she had eyes that were pools of blue. With one hand gripping a wooden support, she looked a little lost. In my view this woman was the best, certainly the most sensitive, writer in America at that time: Carson McCullers. Franco linked arms with these two people of genius, two loners, and enabled them to laugh together, to endure together the life of the outcast and pariah, the life of the scapegoat and misfit, a life familiar at that time to every American artist and non-conformist.

Tennessee Williams preferred the company of men in his bed to that of women. Carson's husband had committed suicide not long before, and she was half-paralyzed. Franco liked both men and women, but he preferred Tennessee. And he also loved poor, sick, tired Carson very dearly. All the poetry, all the suns of the world proved incapable of lighting up her blue eyes, of animating her heavy eyelids and gaunt body. But she kept her laugh, the laugh of a child forever lost. I saw how these two men, whom people would then refer to with a kind of prudish distaste as "pederasts" and who nowadays would be described as "gay" (as if they should somehow be cheerful when they are despised by every Tom, Dick and Harry for loving the way they do), I saw how they took care of this woman, putting her to bed, getting her up, dressing her, entertaining her, warming her, loving her—in short, giving her all that friendship and understanding and attentiveness can offer to someone who is too sensitive, who has seen too much and learned too much from what she has seen, and perhaps written too much about it, to be able to bear it or endure it any longer.

Carson was to die ten years later, and Franco not long afterwards. As for Tennessee—by then the writer perhaps most hated by puritans, but most acclaimed by the public and by critics—the author of *A Streetcar Named Desire, Cat on a Hot Tin Roof, The Night of the Iguana,* and many other plays died a miserable death in a hotel room in New York which he left wide open, rain or shine. He was a man who liked to laugh and laughed heartily, and sometimes very tenderly. I never really found out why or how he died—unless perhaps it was Carson's death, and then Franco's, and then the deaths of so many others that I didn't know about, that finally killed him. But he was a good man. Like Sartre and Giacometti, and a few other men I have known only too little, he was totally incapable of being hurtful, aggressive or harsh. He was good and he was manly. And what does it matter that he preferred being good and manly with young men at night since he was both those things with the whole of the human race during the day.

So we spent a torrid and riotous two weeks in Key West, which was deserted at that time of year. This was twenty-five years ago. More than twenty-five years ago. In the morning we would meet on the beach. Carson and Tennessee used to drink tumblers full of water—or what I took for such until I finally swallowed a large mouthful and realized it was straight gin. We went swimming, we hired little rowboats, we tried in vain to catch big fish. The men drank, and the women too, only a little less. We had truly awful picnics. And after these really memorable outings we would go home tired, sometimes happy, sometimes sad, but happy or sad together.

I can still see Carson in those incredible Bermuda shorts that were too long for her, with her long arms, her little bowed head and short hair, and her eyes such a pale blue they made her look a child once more. I can see Tennessee's profile as he read the paper, laughing occasionally—because otherwise, he used to say, it would have

made him weep (at that time I took very little interest in politics). I can see Franco making his way
along the beach, coming down the steps, going
to fetch glasses, running from one to the other,
laughing; Italian, well-built, not handsome but
charming, Franco was light-hearted, droll, good,
full of imagination.

Apart from Carson and myself, I think they had
very few visitors at their house in Duncan Street.
It was a two- or three-bedroom house, and Tennessee had turned one of the rooms into a study.
There he would type for hours, apparently unaware of the terrific heat out on the patio. There
was a garden, and a large black woman—straight
out of a film—would be watering it. And then there
were the three of us—three admiring French people who perhaps got in the way, but who were so
happy to be there that sometimes the mere sight
of us would make them all burst out laughing. I
said very little to any of them. We did not discuss
anything very profound. We did not talk about our
private lives, we were quite reserved with one another, but I knew then that one day I would look
back regretfully on those moments of happiness.

Two or three years later I came across Tennessee
again. It was the day of a presidential election and
so the blue laws were in force. We sat once more

at the bar in the Hotel Pierre, where he very coolly ordered two glasses, ice and a bottle of lemonade, then took out of his back pocket a flask of strong whisky from which he poured me a typically generous measure. His latest play was doing very well, but he did not mention it. He was sad, because Carson was sad; because Carson had had to return for a while to a hospital—for "the highly strung," as he put it—and he said this with the utmost conviction. He was sad because Carson had then left this institution, supposedly recovered, but now she was staying in the large house where she had spent her childhood, to be with her mother, who was dying of cancer. She was pleased to hear I was in New York, and Tennessee had promised that we would drive out and see her the following day.

So we set out, all three of us—Franco, Tennessee and I—one sparkling golden autumn day, one of those Indian summer days that you get in New York. And in a little old rattletrap of an MG, a small convertible that Tennessee had at the time, we drove across part of Connecticut, or New Jersey, I don't know which—in any event a splendidly beautiful place with red trees, though in the midst of all the beauty was a sign on the front of some private club that read "No jews, no dogs." And the sight of it was like a slap across the face.

We were just a dozen miles out of New York—it seemed to me insane. Franco broke the silence by starting to sing Italian songs at the top of his voice.

We were still singing when we arrived at the home of Carson McCullers, author of master-pieces such as *The Heart Is a Lonely Hunter, Reflections in a Golden Eye,* works that have only gradually become known in France. It was an old porticoed house with three steps and all the doors were open because of the heat. Sitting on a divan was a very old, anemic-looking lady, ravaged by suffering or something else which set her apart and made her almost disdainful of our presence. And then there was Carson, wearing a brown dress thrown on any old way; Carson, grown even thinner and paler, but who still had those eyes, those extraordinary eyes, and that childlike laugh.

We set about opening bottles, and Carson's mother made a show of consenting to have a drop only after being pressed upon to do so. We drank a lot. The weather had become really cold by the time we drove back and the return journey in the car was a sad one, despite the fact that we were heading for that galaxy of a city, that enormous place where every city dweller knew their names by heart, yet knew nothing of their souls. Unfortunately, as it turned out, it was not even a month later, just a week, in fact, before Carson had to go back to that place where they look after the highly strung. Neither Tennessee nor even Franco could raise a smile after that . . .

And yet the circumstances could not have been more jolly when I came upon both of them in Rome, a year later, at one of those cocktail parties that Americans like to throw for the Italians. Faulkner was there. He left after a short time in amorous pursuit of a very young and beautiful blonde in whom he seemed at once madly interested and as if he couldn't care less. We made our escape and went off to meet Anna Magnani with whom we were to have dinner. "La Magnani" was raging against men, the whole male population. One of her lovers had treated her badly the day before—I don't remember the details—and she was still angry. She remained angry the whole evening. All of Franco's jokes, all his wild laughter, even after Tennessee and I joined in, failed to calm her down. She did not even laugh when a whore, a friend of Franco, called out to us gaily, or rather to him, pleadingly: "*E quando Franco? Quando, quando, quando?*"

"Soon," he said, maneuvering the car to avoid several cyclists and a bus. "Soon, darling, I'll be with you soon."

He raised his hand and smiled at the girl, and

she smiled back, and Tennessee, who was sitting in the back of the car, also smiled into his moustache, as if he were observing his rogue of a son chatting up a young girl. There was a great deal of tenderness between them, a very great deal.

And then one evening, a long time after, I was back in New York, at one of those intellectual parties I had yet again unwisely chanced to attend. And there I saw a man who was a mere shadow of his former self.

Tennessee had grown gray, thin, transparent. His eyes had lost their blueness; his blond moustache was gone, and so too was the hearty laugh. He hugged me with a kind of desperation that was close to resentment. At first I could not understand the meaning of it all, until at last someone had the goodness to tell me: on no account should Franco be mentioned, because— "Really, it's such a stupid story"—Tennessee had quarreled with Franco and had gone away for six months to India or somewhere, to spend some time without him; to convince himself he was right, or simply in an attempt to score points, or perhaps because both of them had tried too often to score points. And when he got back from those exotic places that fate had led him to visit, where the mail never arrived, the first thing he learned was that Franco was dying; he had been very ill for three months, all the while thinking he had fallen out with Tennessee, constantly asking for him, and waiting for him to come back.

Since then Tennessee had been a broken man. He no longer laughed. He held me by the hand in a corner of the bar; but his hand was limp, and his holding mine was a friendly gesture made out of habit, or perhaps because he had a vague memory of having held my hand before. I left thinking that I would never see him again, since he was flanked by two barbaric-looking individuals sporting glasses, certificates and beards, who dogged his every footstep, hung on every word he uttered, helped him to food and drink—and especially pills. They looked more like Mafia heavies than well-meaning specialists of despair.

And then—it must have been about twelve years ago—André Barsacq, who was director of the Théâtre Atelier, had an open "slot," as they say, in the autumn program. At the last minute he asked me to adapt a play for him, it didn't matter who by. André Barsacq was responsible for an endless succession of disasters, triumphs, failures and resounding comebacks. I liked him very much, and I told him then and there that Tennessee Williams was the only writer who might tempt me to resurrect and reactivate my English, as faltering as ever—despite years without schooling or the services of an English professor! We checked his bookings and files and the various dates of performances, and decided on *Sweet Bird of Youth,* which had already played in New York and been quite a success. It had also been made into a film with Paul Newman and Geraldine Page. There was, of course, no translation of the play, or none that Tennessee liked. It was up to me to have a go at it.

I began in May or June with someone who spoke English fluently to help me, and I worked as I have never in my life worked since, that is to say, nonstop, slaving and agonizing over every word, losing patience, feeling overwhelmed with shame or pleasure, passing through the various stages that enabled me to enter a little into Tennessee's poetic world.

His text was stark and beautiful, very stark and very beautiful, with moments of tenderness and savagery. Sometimes the voice of a single man, a single phrase, could unleash the dogs of passion. And at times in the gentle-spoken woman there was the ferocity of a praying mantis. There were the murders; the town; the recurring memories of youth and childhood. And there was the other woman, the actress whose childhood was so far behind her, and the boy, a two-bit gigolo, who,

besides the cocktail shakers and Vuitton suit-
cases, had to fetch and carry strange pills, oxy-
gen masks, creams and facial treatments and who,
from time to time, if he were in a good mood,
would slip into the bed where she was waiting to
rob him of his youth to keep it for herself—if only
for a single night. And there were the two of them,
afterward, saying to each other the craziest, the
cruelest and at times the most noble things you
were ever likely to hear.

All that hot summer I was amazed by the
amount of work I did. I would go back over a
phrase twenty or thirty times, something I have
never done, though it's probably a mistake, for any
of my own plays. I delivered the script on time.
Edwige Feuillère played the main part and gave a
spellbinding performance. The sets were designed by Jacques Dupont and were splendid.

Of course we had alerted Tennessee to what
we were about, right from the start, but I was
thunderstruck when we received a telegram from
him three days before the opening: "I'M ON MY WAY."
I raced over to his hotel. It was a luxury hotel,
which surprised me, because I knew that he had
financial problems, and that for some bizarre reason—to me, a Frenchwoman, it seemed insane—
America had rejected him. Apparently he was now
thought of as someone who had once known how
to tell a good story, and had been lucky in finding

good actors able to interpret his confused scripts. Period. In other words, he was well on the way to being penniless. He was not the kind of man given to saving money, and with a picture in mind of the furtive and silent ghost I had last glimpsed in some skyscraper in New York, I was a bit anxious about the idea of seeing my friend Tennessee again, and nearly in tears to think of him taking the trouble to come all the way. I prepared myself for the worst, knowing just how badly things can go wrong for somebody already down. I imagined the play a total flop, the audience hissing wildly, the acting terrible, my translation sounding hideous to him—and that this could be the last straw for such a tender and fragile man.

And yet the Tennessee I encountered was exactly the same as the person I had known in Key West fifteen years earlier. He had grown his moustache again. He had the same blue eyes and loud laugh, and he was followed everywhere—like a patient by some ultrastylish nurse—by a certain countess from the very best of English society who had become enamoured of Tennessee's talent and personal charm, as I imagine Madame von Meck had been with Tchaikovsky. But unlike Madame von Meck, the countess did not let her author out of her sight. Tennessee found this role of "very dear friend" highly amusing. "Very dear, but not too dear, you see," he would say, and he who had always dispensed his millions with gay abandon seemed sometimes surprised that, now that his circumstances had been reversed, only he and I of the assembled company could really appreciate the joke.

For the first act we were hidden away in a box. Tennessee sat beside me, wide-eyed, and at first he listened; then he began to laugh, but so loudly, at lines that were indeed supposed to be funny, that people turned around in their seats to see who was making the noise. And the lower I sank in my seat, the louder he laughed, until in the end I leaned over toward him and said:

"But it's not that funny."

"Ah, but it is," he said. "You don't realize just how funny. I was really very funny in those days."

And he laughed like a madman. He was even asked not to make so much noise, though the usherettes, baffled once they recognized the translator and playwright—two people who by the law of the theatre ought to be haunting the wings with lugubrious demeanor, as they might the gangways of a steamer about to go down, and certainly not causing this kind of ruckus—left us alone. We calmed down during intermission— naturally everybody who was anybody was there. Tennessee cast a bemused eye over the assembly and rushed out into the rue des Abbesses, a street of notorious ill-repute—to be precise, the haunt of boys, of men, the hard and the pliant, one of those districts in Clichy in which a woman has little reason to go wandering at night, let alone venture into its obscure recesses. Nevertheless, with three brave men among our number, we sallied forth; after all, we had to find Tennessee so that we could introduce him to the audience. We finally tracked him down in the depths of the most sinister-looking dive, as happy as a lark, eating some unrecognizable dish spiced with garlic or God-knows-what-other earthy flavoring, and I suddenly had a vision of the refined little candlelit dinner that would be served in the sumptuous suite of the English countess's luxury hotel. But I won't dwell on that.

The audience applauded enthusiastically. Tennessee was unwillingly brought out onto the stage. He too clapped enthusiastically, which made everyone laugh and clap twice as loudly as before. We left in a state of euphoria, some of us in the countess's Rolls, the rest in their own cars, and drove to the celebrated suite in that well-known establishment whose name I have forgotten, where Tennessee hugged me in a corner good-naturedly and told me that I was "the dearest girl," and that my translation was splendid. Even though his French was still not very good, there were lots of things that he had liked very much indeed—and he was pleased that I too should understand such things. It was all said very quickly and in that muddled way authors fall back on when talking to each other about their own works.

"So you didn't feel too greatly betrayed?" I asked, the only question that had been obsessing me since the whole thing began.

"No, darling, I felt loved. More than anything, you understand. Loved."

And he hugged me once again, before rushing after a glass of alcohol he had just seen carried before his eyes, but which had escaped the countess's notice.

That was the last time I saw him. I heard later about his escapades at the Cannes Film Festival, and about his absolute refusal to preside a minute longer in that particular capitalist Court of Miracles. I laughed about it, but the joke was on me, since it was my fate to succeed him a few years later, and I had more or less the same feelings about it as he did. (But that's neither here nor there.) Whether I think of the fair-haired, suntanned man with blue eyes and a blond moustache who carried Carson McCullers up to her bedroom, laid her against her two pillows like a child, sat at the foot of her bed and held her hand until she fell asleep because she was afraid of nightmares; or the gray-faced wreck of Tennessee, drained of life by the irrevocable loss of

Franco; or the Tennessee who so kindly came such a long way and probably thought our staging of his play to be like some pantomime in a village hall but nevertheless had the goodness and gallantry to say the opposite—I shall always miss the unvarying directness of his gaze, his unvarying strength, tenderness, vulnerability.

"I felt that you loved me, darling, I know that you loved my play." And I don't even know how you died, my poor poet. I don't know what indignities were heaped upon you in New York before, or after, or since then. I don't know whether you ended up yearning for that bizarre death at dawn in an open house, and whether perhaps you arranged it. Or maybe you were calmly thinking of going and spending a few days in that house in Florida—probably mortgaged—with the sun, the beach and the dark nights; with your friends, your writing paper—what drama in a blank piece of paper!—in your room, the room where you would withdraw in the afternoons, with or without a bottle, and from which you would later emerge, slim, young, delivered, triumphant—a poet, no less. I miss you, poet, and I fear I shall miss you for a long time to come.

Speeding

The plane trees at the side of the road seem to lie flat; at night the neon lights of gas stations are lengthened and distorted; your tires no longer screech, but are suddenly muffled and quietly attentive; even your sorrows are swept away: however madly and hopelessly in love you may be, at 120 miles an hour you are less so. Your blood no longer congeals around your heart; your blood throbs to the extremities of your body; to your fingertips, your toes and your eyelids, now the fateful and tireless guardians of your own life. It's crazy how your body, your nerves and your senses hold you in the grip of life. For who has not thought that life was pointless without that other person, and put his foot down on an accelerator at once responsive and resistant? Who has not then felt his whole body tense, his right hand move to stroke the gears while his left hand grips the steering wheel, legs outstretched, deceptively relaxed, but ready for a violent jolt, ready to swerve and brake? And while taking all these precautions to remain alive, who has not thrilled to the awesome and fascinating silence of imminent death, at once a rebuttal and a provocation? Whoever has not thrilled to speed has not thrilled to life—or perhaps has never loved anyone.

First, there is, outside, this metal animal, to all eyes quietly sleeping, though you can wake it with a turn of a magic key. It coughs; you allow it to catch its breath, recover its voice and come to grips with another day, just as you would a friend who has woken too quickly. You gently propel this animal in the direction of the town and its streets, or the countryside and its lanes. Its engine gradually warms up, settling down to its own pace, slowly becoming excited by what it sees just as you do: fields or embankments, whichever, smooth surfaces to glide over and shoot along, bettering previous performance. You glance past cars to right and left, or, impatiently, mark time behind some debilitated road hog just in front of you. And then there's the same reflex: left foot down, wrist up a little, and with a slight jerk your car surges forward and overtakes the one in front, then settles down to a gently purring pace. This metal box flows through the arteries of the city and slips between its banks, emerging into squares, as if circulating in some vast vascular system it has no wish to block. Or this same metal box rolls through the countryside in the morning emerging from curtains of fog to rosy fields and shadowy borders, with the added danger of a steep incline now and again; the car stutters and again your left foot goes down and your right hand moves up and there is a joyous uphill surge, the small challenge of the climb causing the car to complain, but as soon as the road levels out it recovers its even rhythm. You are completely in control. The noises the car makes are subtly pleasing to the ear and to your body. There is no jolting, and you disdain to use the brakes. You are an eye above all else, the eye of the driver of this metal creature, an exquisite, highly strung creature that is useful but lethal—and what does that matter? You are an attentive, confident, mistrustful, busy, casual eye; motionless but quick, searching for someone else, making a desperate effort, not to find this other person now lost forever, but, on the contrary, to avoid any encounter.

At night the car shoots out of a bend into minefields, into fields strewn with the unforeseen, misleading lights and blinding yellow arcs across the sky; your headlights pick out what masquerade as wide roadways at the bottoms of ditches, and a host of other traps lie where the ground falls away at the edge of your high beams; and there are all these unknown human beings you drive past, striking them as they connive to strike you with all the violence of the air between you forced out by your passing cars. All these unidentified drivers, all these enemies who dazzle you, leaving you dazed and disoriented on some asphalt strip beneath the furtive and deceptive moonlight. And sometimes you feel terribly drawn to the right, toward the trees that line the road, or to the left and the oncoming traffic—you want to escape somewhere, somehow, to avoid their raging headlights.

And there are those rest stops, all concrete, soda and small change, where highway adventurers take refuge, having escaped the domination of their own instinctive reflexes. And how quiet and peaceful it is there. It seems the black coffee you drank there could easily have been your last, the trailers on the road at Auxerre were so crazy, and you yourself could hardly see the road in front of you, what with the hailstorm and ice. Every one of the countless modest heroes of the highway is so used to brushes with death that it doesn't occur to him to make an issue of it. He just keeps going, driving along, eyes blinking in the headlights, his imagination working on what might happen. Is he going to overtake that car now? Do I have time to get by? His hands are ice-cold, sometimes his heart stops beating. You come across these cautious, silent heroes every night on the highway and at truck stops; they are in a hurry, tired, dogged, above all worried because it is still some sixty miles from Lyons to Valence, or Paris to Rouen, and after Mantes or Chalon there are only so many places you can stop, and so many places to tank up. So you take advantage of these stopovers and pull out of the game for five minutes. Still in one piece, safe in the shadow of the station billboard, you sit there watching the cars that were following you, or that you overtook in the past hour, drive past like kamikaze pilots. And there you take a deep breath, acting as if you will be in these temporary—so very temporary—refuges for good, refuges you will have to leave even if you become suddenly afraid of the black monsters to the rear and in front of you, and of their violent glaring beams that pierce the night and madden you. Then you take hold of yourself, or what's left of you and your machine; the engine moans and purrs and carries you off—you at the mercy of your engine, the engine at yours. And when you are back in your seat on your own plastic or leather cushion, with the smell of your own cigarettes, as your warm quick hand touches the cold wood or Bakelite of the steering wheel that has brought you this far and will, with luck, take you farther on your travels, then you know that a car is not just a means of transport but also an object of mythic proportions, possibly the instrument of your Destiny, capable of bringing about your downfall or your salvation; it is Hippolytus's chariot, and not the ten thousandth replica off a production line.

Contrary to what one might think, the tempos of speed are not those of music. It is not the *allegro, vivace,* or *furioso* in a symphony which corresponds to 120 miles an hour, but the *andante,* the slow, majestic movement, a sort of plateau that you reach above a certain speed, when the car no longer protests, when there is no acceleration, just the opposite, in fact; the car and your body drift in harmony into a sort of alert and attentive state of giddiness, normally described as intoxicating. This sort of thing happens at night on a road in the middle of nowhere, and sometimes during the day in deserted places. When it happens the words "prohibited," "fasten seatbelts," "social security," "hospital," "death" no longer have any meaning, have been simply wiped out by a single word that men have used throughout the ages, a word that describes a silver racing car or a chestnut horse: the word "speed." The kind of speed you reach when something inside you outstrips something exterior to your body; that moment when the indomitable violence of a machine breaks loose or when an animal reverts to its wild state, and all your intelligence and sensibility and skill—and sensuality too—are barely able to control it; certainly your control is so tenuous there's still room for pleasure, and still room for the possibility such pleasure will prove fatal. Ours is a hateful age in which risk, the unpredictable, the illogical are constantly rejected, held up against numbers and deficits and calculations; it is a mean-spirited age that forbids people to kill themselves not because of the immeasurable value of their souls but because of the immediately computable price of their carcasses.

The truth of the matter is that a car—your car—endows you as its slave and master with the paradoxical sensation of being free at last, of returning to the maternal bosom, to an original state of solitude, far from alien eyes. Neither pedestrians, nor policemen, nor fellow motorists, nor the woman who might be waiting for him, nor all of life that waits for no man can separate the driver from his car, the only one of his possessions, after all, which allows him, for an hour a day, to rediscover in tangible form the solitude he was born to. And if the waves of traffic divide before the driver's car like the Red Sea before the Israelites; if red lights occur at greater intervals, more and more infrequently, until they disappear altogether; and if the road begins to shimmy and whisper in response to his foot on the accelerator; if the wind tears past his door like a hurricane; if each bend is a danger and a surprise, and each mile marks a small victory—why be surprised that imperturbable bureaucrats destined for brilliant careers within their companies should go and immolate themselves in glorious pirouettes of metal and gravel and blood, in final celebration of their terrestrial nature and ultimate defiance of what the future holds for them? These somersaults are described as accidents; loss of concentration, absent-mindedness are offered as explanations—everything except the most important reason, which is the exact opposite of these. It is the sudden unanticipated and irresistible fusion of body and soul, when a human being has an abrupt and fleeting insight into the nature of existence: Who on earth am I? I am myself, I am alive, this is what living means. I travel at fifty miles an hour through towns, seventy on main roads, eighty on highways, three hundred in my mind, though it feels like three in my skin—all in accordance with the highway code, the conventions of society and the laws of despair. What are these meaningless scales of numbers which have dogged me since childhood? Why should the speed of my life be dictated to me, when one life is all I have . . .

But now we digress from the idea of pleasure, of speed as pleasure, which, when all is said and done, is the best definition. And let me say it straight out, like Morand, like Proust, like Dumas: there is nothing imprecise, formless or shameful about this pleasure. It is a clearly defined, exultant and almost serene pleasure to drive too fast, exceeding the limitations of the car and the surface on which you are driving, exceeding the car's capacity to hold the road and perhaps even your own reflexes. And let me be clear that this is not a wager against oneself, nor an idiotic challenge to one's own skill; it is no showdown of self against self, or victory over some personal impediment. It is, rather, a lighthearted gamble between oneself and pure chance. When you go fast there is a moment when everything begins to float inside this metal vessel, when you reach the razor's edge, the crest of the wave, and you hope to come down on the right side, thanks not so much to your skill as to the direction of the current. A taste for speed has nothing to do with sport. Just as speed is tied with the idea of risk-taking and chance, so too is it tied to the joy of being alive, and therefore the vague death wish of which there is always a trace where there is *joie de vivre*. Well, that is everything that I believe to be true—speed is neither signal, nor proof, nor provocation, nor challenge; it is a surge of happiness.

Orson Welles

For two months I had been taking refuge in Grassin, an exquisite little village in the hills some 600
feet above sea level, which for the past thirty years
has cast a reproving eye down on the excesses of
its mad sister, Saint-Tropez. It had been raining
for two months, and what with evenings round the
fireplace and excursions to the bistro on the corner, it seemed to me more like the Sologne than
the Midi. It was in 1959, or '60, or '61, I don't remember now: once out of adolescence, the years
begin to stack up, happy or unhappy, and I have

---

become incapable of keeping track of them. I had just walked out on my husband for the first time, but I was nevertheless still well enough disposed toward men in general to promise a very close male friend, who was involved in the Cannes Film Festival, to meet up with him there one day.

All I knew about Cannes and the Film Festival was the image most people had of the place at that time—that is to say, a blend of chilled champagne, warm sea, an admiring crowd and American demigods—and I confess that the mix did not greatly appeal to me. My reservations turned out to be well-founded, for we had no sooner arrived and perched ourselves on the steps of the old Palais du Festival to watch the judges and the stars of the day as they entered than I was suddenly swept along in a wild surge forward of the crowd, provoked by the arrival of Anita Ekberg, or Gina Lollobrigida, or someone similar and which transformed the docile and wide-eyed bystanders into a wildly impatient horde. I myself am not usually frightened by people, but on this occasion, with faces and glimpses of faces and shoulders all around me, and chasms of blackness alternating with patches of brilliant sunshine, I confess that I was seized with panic. I flailed around, and was about to succumb to the force of numbers, as the silly expression goes, when a tremendously powerful arm pulled me out of that hell and carried me along stairways, corridors, and through secret doors to an office where I was lowered onto a sofa. It was then that I discovered that this kindly King Kong was also the King Kong of seduction; even before I set eyes on him, I recognized his laugh and knew it was Orson Welles.

Sitting in that office, if I remember correctly, were—apart from a few officials involved in the festival and my totally bewildered friend—Darryl Zanuck and Juliette Greco, together with an impresario friend. Once the initial formalities were over and the first restorative whisky had been drunk, he suggested we all have dinner together that evening at the Bonne Auberge. As far as I was concerned, he might have suggested dinner in Valparaiso or Lille; as long as Welles was going to be there, there was no question but I would follow. There were very few illusions about men that I had managed to lose but these had been instantly revived by his mere presence. He was huge, a real colossus, and his eyes were yellow, his laugh thunderous. He gazed on the port of Cannes, with its frenzied crowds and sumptuous yachts, with the jaundiced, wary amusement of an outsider.

During the years that followed I would recount this anecdote whenever the conversation turned to Welles, and I reached a point where I began to wonder whether it had really taken place; each of us has a selective memory that sorts through our experiences, preserving the good times and forgetting the bad—or vice versa—and occasionally our imagination will condescend to lend a hand. I saw Welles again years later in Paris, in the Luxembourg Gardens, where he came to meet me for lunch, and it was only when he tucked me under his arm like a bundle of laundry—on the pretext that he didn't want me to be crushed—and carried me, shouting and cursing, along the streets, with my head and feet hanging down on either side of his arm, that I could finally believe my first memories of him were accurate. But that's another story . . .

To return to Cannes, and the year I have failed to pinpoint—it was the year they showed *Touch of Evil*—we did indeed have dinner at the Bonne Auberge. There was my friend, a love-smitten Zanuck, a wisecracking Greco, and a debt-ridden Welles. Lack of funds had brought shooting to a halt halfway through his last film, and it was more or less understood that this dinner was to persuade Darryl Zanuck (already one of the most powerful Hollywood producers) to come to the rescue. For about half an hour, I think, it was a fairly quiet meal; the hors d'oeuvres, a specialty of the restaurant, succeeded one another in choreographed sequence, and we discussed the afternoon's adventures in Franglais. Everyone laughed, everyone was amusing. And then the conversation turned inevitably to motion pictures in general, then to producing, and then to the role of the producer in filmmaking, and from that point on everyone spoke English, and more and more quickly. I confess that I listened politely, but not very closely, and then I was suddenly thrown forward into my plate by a vigorous slap on the back from the person sitting on my left—Orson himself.

"You and I," he said, "are artists. We have nothing in common with this mob of financiers and cheap crooks. They should be avoided like the plague. They're just middlemen, they're . . ."

A few insults followed whose meaning I did not entirely grasp but which proved sufficiently effective to cause Zanuck to turn pale, take his cigar out of his mouth, and get to his feet. Welles left with us, without having eaten his dessert, his film no nearer completion. I was terribly sorry about the movie, yet at the same time thrilled for him. For him, for Life, and Art, for the "artistes," as he called them; for truth, grace, grandeur—whatever you care to mention—and it thrills me still. I did not see him again for ten years, although there were several telephone calls between Grassin, Paris and London to make plans that, alas, came to nothing.

That day, after having toted me like a bag of laundry all round the streets of Paris and the Champs-Elysées, he finally set me down at a table to eat with two friends of his. He ate like a wolf, laughed like an ogre, and we all finished up spending the afternoon in his suite in the George V, which is where he had at last come to rest after a stormy passage through the other luxury hotels of Paris. He paced up and down talking of Shakespeare, of the hotel menu, of the stupidity of the press, and someone or other's depression. I find it impossible to quote a single phrase he uttered. I watched him fascinated. I don't believe there's another person in the world who can so forcefully convey the impression of genius; there is in him such extravagance, vitality, finality, fatefulness, disillusionment and passion. I knew only a moment of terror when, out of the blue, he suggested that we leave in an hour for—where else?— Valparaiso. I was on my way out the door to fetch my passport (ready now to abandon a second marital home, my child, my dog, my cat, and not with dishonorable intentions, but simply because Welles was irresistible and the least of his wishes quite clearly had to be fulfilled). Thank God—or

blame him—the telephone rang, someone re-
minded Welles that he had to go to London, and
the Valparaiso trip never came off.

The following week, still reeling from my encounter with him, I arranged—thanks to *L'Express*, for which I was writing film reviews at the
time—to have all his films screened for me. In the
space of a few days, I saw the four pictures I hadn't
seen before, and all the others again. I confess I
was baffled. I could not understand why the
Americans weren't falling at his feet to offer him
contracts, or why French producers, supposedly
so eager to take risks in this period, were not
rushing off to find him in the English countryside.
Even if it meant assigning him two bodyguards in
the event he showed any sign of leaving the set
(and this did happen from time to time, they say)
for Mexico, or elsewhere, in the middle of filming.

I saw plenty that week: the enormous corpse
of the corrupt police captain, the sadistic cop,
floats amidst the detritus in the water under a
bridge. Marlene Dietrich gazes at it. The honest
lawyer asks her: "Are you going to miss him?"

She replies, "He was some kind of a man."

General Rodriguez studies the photo of the
man she loved, who robbed her and will soon kill
her. "What do you think of him?"

"He was some kind of a man."

A broken Joseph Cotten speaks of the man

who betrayed him and hunted him down, his best friend: "He was some kind of a man."

I could go on. But seeing all these Welles films one after the other, I thought I recognized in all of them the same obsession: an obsession with temperament. Welles likes a certain kind of man, one no doubt like himself: violent, tender, intelligent, amoral, rich; self-obsessed and self-consuming, a force of nature, domineering, fearsome, never understood yet never complaining about it, probably not even concerned about it. The young and ruthless Kane, the arrogant Arkadin, the brooding Othello, all monstrous, all loners—the price of supreme intelligence. There is only one film in which he played the part of the victim—*The Lady from Shanghai.* The role of the monster is left to Rita Hayworth; it must be said that he was in love with her.

Yet this superb solitude became a heavy burden. In order to make a living, Welles was obliged to play some ridiculous parts; he had been deprived of his weapon—his camera. A world of little men with glasses and mechanical pencils, of accountants and producers, had succeeded in overthrowing Gulliver, who had things other than these Lilliputians to occupy his mind. He almost succumbed to the onslaught. Then he made *Touch of Evil.* I was struck by one particularly fine sequence among many others: the point where he again meets the woman who has been as splen-

did a monster as he—Marlene. She tells him that
he has grown fat and ugly, that he looks like
nothing on earth; she tells him that his future is
behind him; and for the first time in any of his
films there is a suggestion of something resembling pity. She blows smoke through her nostrils,
as in *The Blue Angel,* and he has that look of a
wounded bull before the kill. What has happened
to Kane, the young black raging bull who raised
terror in the rings of America? What have they done
to him? What has he done to himself? I did not
know enough of what had been going on to say.
I simply knew that all his films reeked of talent and
that the question that sprang to mind was just who
was played out?

Even so, after that came *The Trial,* and several articles on Welles's technique, his immoder-
ation, his violence, and so on. Anyone who goes
to see any one of his films will find in it poetry,
imagination, elegance, everything which makes for
real cinema. Personally speaking, it is his obses-
sions that interest me. Money, for example. Welles
should have been fabulously wealthy. He would
really have loved to be. Remember that scene in
Mr. Arkadin? The young man is running through
the streets. It's Christmas night and he must find
some *foie gras* to satisfy the absurd whim of an
old man whom he's trying to protect. He stum-
bles against a Rolls belonging to Arkadin, who
wants to kill him but very kindly takes him to a

grand restaurant where fifteen waiters rush to bring Mr. Arkadin *foie gras*. Remember the balls at the Ambersons', Kane's picnic, the Rolls, the châteaus, the airplanes, the yachts, the parties, the hundreds of flunkies, secretaries and good-time girls. What a shame! What a shame Welles did not buy shares in Shell or set up a chain of snackbars with the fruits of his early successes. What a shame that he wandered around the world squandering his money! What a pity he did not invest in anything other than his own will and pleasure. I do not intend any irony. For not only would he have his Rolls, he would also have had a production company, and we would be able to see a masterpiece every three years . . .

What a pity for us and certainly for him, yet what a splendid destiny this genius enjoys, living from day to day, visiting Paris to get decorated by Mitterrand, returning to a farm in America to nurse his arthritis, making commercials for absurd sums of money. What a fine figure of a man he is, immense in every way, yet condemned to live among dwarfs with no imagination and no soul. With royal disdain he manages to extort from them just enough to feed and water his carcass. No one will ever be able to make a film about Welles. At least I hope not. Because no one in the world could have his stature, his face, or especially his eyes, whose unrelenting brilliance is the hallmark of a genius.

The Theatre

I began my theatrical career for the most natural and most modest of reasons: to entertain my friends. I had rented a charming house that winter, forty miles from Paris, where I could go through one of my anti-frivolous periods: enough of life in Paris, enough of nightclubs, whisky, love affairs, and painting the town red—it's time for reading, log fires, classical music and philosophical discussions. These crises have always come at regular intervals to shake up my life, or rather, to calm it down for a while. This particular crisis occurred in the course of writing my third book. I had very selfishly buried myself, along with my characters, in the final pages. I had not noticed the last autumn leaves fall; not even the snow had distracted me. I had not noticed that the days had grown shorter and my friends' faces longer. When I regained consciousness, so to speak, after writing the words "The End" to *Those Without Shadows*, I saw all around me nothing but nervous breakdowns, lovesickness, spiritual unease, and other vexations that people of all ages suffer, but which are especially rife among city-dwellers exiled in the country. The sight of pen and paper still acting as a stimulus to my brain and prompting my hand, I wrote Act I, Scene 1 of a play, and thereby began a dialogue between a brother and sister snowbound in winter in a château in Sweden. No doubt I vaguely hoped that the comparison between this fate and their own would restore a degree of optimism to my friends. In any event, this beginning of an act made them laugh. (And it was no sycophantic laughter: I have always kept company with wonderful but intractable friends, who are no less intractable when it comes to reading my books. And I generally come in more for unflattering critiques than cries of admiration. As for the obsequious court of enthusiastic and mindless parasites which has sometimes been attributed to me, I confess there are days when I have positively longed for it.)

In fact it isn't true that this was my first venture into the theatre. I clearly remember that, from the age of only twelve, I would inundate my mother with historical and melodramatic plays, and that even in bed she could not escape my reading them aloud to her.

They were in the following vein:

THE KING: Throw him into the deepest dungeon . . .

THE QUEEN: Sire, have mercy. You have not the right . . .

THE PRISONER: Madame, desist. I shall die as I have lived: on my feet.

THE KING (sneering): On your feet! Ha! On your knees in the straw, rather.

THE QUEEN: Sire, you are not a cruel man, I know . . . How can you . . . et cetera.

Despite her immense graciousness, my mother would slowly wilt after half an hour of such bombastic exchanges. I could see her eyes become unfocused, narrow, then disappear beneath eyelids that provided welcome escape. Then

I would sigh and get up, feeling a mixture of tenderness and compassion; of course it was a fairly difficult text, fairly violent, fairly strong stuff, in fact, and I had perhaps been wrong to spring it on my mother like that, in between two fashionable dinner parties—catching her sensibilities unaware, and subjecting her so abruptly to the impact of Literature and Drama. The way I saw it, she had not actually gone to sleep. She had, as it were, taken refuge in sleep, to escape the verbal violence she had not known her child to possess. One day, soon, she would be weeping in the third row in the front stalls, along with the rest of fashionable Paris, petrified with fear and admiration.

And I would go and rest my even then untidy hair on a soft pillow, safe in the bosom of my family, and fall asleep almost instantaneously—but not without having had visions of Act II.

Anyway, that winter I had already embarked on a "literary career," as they say, with two books published and a third completed; and who, after all, was going to stop my dreaming of the theatre? No one, of course. And no one else can be blamed for my then recklessly driving my convertible into a field. I was given the last rites there and then, presumed dying, and for six months, wherever I went, I was dressed only in bandages.

What happened next was completely fortui-
tous. A year later Jacques Brenner, editor of a little magazine called *Le Cahier des Saisons,* asked
me for some unpublished material, and sheer la-
ziness prompted me to send him what I had to
hand—the beginning of that Swedish act. He published those few pages in his review, and André
Barsacq, who was then running the Théâtre de
l'Atelier, came across it by chance on a train trip.
He was sufficiently taken with it to call me in Paris.
The project was by then two years old, and I was
at first stunned by his enthusiastically talking about
it as if it were a discovery. He came to see me,
told me those thirty pages were very good, but that
it needed another hundred. There had to be a
middle, an end, a plot, a denouement, et cetera—none of which I'd given any thought to,
preoccupied as I'd been at the time simply with
the idea of making my friends laugh.

So I went to Switzerland, to the most mourn-
ful place imaginable, and amid two chalets and
three *Gasthäuser,* amid the snowfall, the fon-
dues, liters and liters of wine and bars of white
chocolate, suddenly all I could think of, as though
it were my last hope, was that play. It had become symbolic for me too; I was, like my protag-
onists, cut off by deep snow, imprisoned among
exceedingly healthy people: cheerful sporty types
with red noses, who indulged in horrendously

hearty après-ski get-togethers. Here I was, cut off far from any kind of fast or degenerate living.

So I wrote *Château in Sweden* in three weeks, and during that time had some mad and sometimes hilarious telephone conversations with André Barsacq. I discovered not how difficult but how easy it is to write for the theatre. For you are guided along, as if on rails, by the demands of the theatre: the unity of time and place; the impossibility of not pursuing the action, since otherwise your audience will lose interest; the need to be swift, to race toward the denouement rather than get lost in sentimental reveries; the overriding necessity of being terse and convincing. All this seemed to correspond exactly with a certain aspect of my temperament as a writer.

Apparently short stories and plays have always been considered more difficult than the novel, the first being considered the fruit of a more subtle art, the second of a more meticulous craft. Yet speaking for myself, I've always felt that my short stories came about from my running out of steam, while plays were the product of an aptitude for dialogue. Short stories and plays are based on characters established from the start; these characters bring about some action which develops quickly and reaches an inevitable climax that is predictable from the opening lines. Whereas the novel wanders from uncertainty to uncertainty, from suggestion to suggestion, from change of character to change of character. In short, the novel permits all the perilous and fatally seductive freedom from constraint, permits all the sidetracking and digressions which must automatically be avoided in a short piece of writing or a dramatic work. You could say that short stories and drama are axioms, and that the novel is an extensive and complex theorem.

Anyway, I wrote *Château in Sweden*, Barsacq staged it, and it was a success. I went to rehearsals several times; in fact every day, as opening night approached, so enchanted was I to hear my words, my thoughts and lines being spoken by real people. I saw the birth of Sebastian in Claude Rich's performance, of Hugo in Philippe Noiret, Eleonore in Françoise Brion, and so on. I watched entranced as these people whom I did not know, who owed me nothing, submitted themselves to the whims of my imagination. I felt extremely grateful toward them. And I must say that even today I still experience the same astonishment and gratitude whenever I see adults delivering words I have written, however funny or not, profound or not, in front of a supposedly adult audience, or one which has at least gone out of its way and paid a small fortune to hear them. I don't think an author ever gets used to that. For me the conviction and evident sincerity with which actors, however great or limited their experience, say out loud these lines that I remember having dreamed up at the end of a rainy afternoon, or after drinking one whisky too many, or after a sudden and questionable flash of inspiration—words I have written *sotto voce,* so to speak—for me this conviction seems born of a reckless dedication to their craft.

So I discovered that year the charms of theatrical success—the applause at times, at other moments the silence—the charms of an audience I thought worth its weight in gold because it had liked my play. And I thrilled to hear what people were saying: "What's more, she can write plays!"

In the meantime I had also become acquainted with "the Theatre"—a theatre that was red and black and gold, with curtains, bouquets of flowers, bottles of champagne, noisy outbursts, surprises, a grand style, and of all this one woman was the apotheosis, Marie Bell, a woman who continues to be the apotheosis of all these things. Well, one fine day, Marie Bell buttonholed me at the hairdresser's. Like some Visigoth queen from beneath her helmet-like dryer, in a voice that thundered all the more loudly since she couldn't hear herself speak, she ordered me to write a play for the Théâtre du Gymnase. I instantly agreed, having also instantly acquired the habit of saying "yes" to Marie—which will surprise no one who knows her. For those who know her less well, let me remind you that she is dark, beautiful and fierce, with eyes like a hawk and an earthy sense of humor. She recites Racine as naturally as the rest of us drink water, and has played prostitutes and empresses equally brilliantly.

And so I wrote a play for Marie Bell, a play entitled *And Sometimes Violins,* which we rehearsed in her majestic theatre for three months, with Pierre Vaneck and an English director whose name I can no longer recall, but who was visibly terrified of Marie Bell. The night of the opening, the audience seemed to me less attentive than they had been for *Château in Sweden.* On Marie's advice, I had submitted to being elaborately made up by one of the top stylists of the day, and huddled in the depths of my box, my eyes stinging with makeup and anxiety, I kept rubbing bright red and black all over my face, so that at intermission several people who knew me comparatively well asked me the way to the dressing rooms, and some even tipped me a few francs as they handed me their coats. I ran and hid under Marie's wing. Although she knew we were heading for a disaster, she tapped her foot and put on a brave face

before plunging into the second act, which con-
firmed our first impression—it was a complete
flop. By a stroke of sheer good luck, *Adieu, Prudence (Farewell to Caution)* by Barillet and Grédy
was alternating at the Gymnase with our *Violins*
and because both were playing alternately like that,
we remained on the bill for several months, although we put on only seventeen performances,
I believe it was.

I won't dwell on the displays of friendship, af-
fection, commiseration—and even the jubilation
of some people—which awaited us at the end of
that painful opening night. The next day Marie Bell
and I went to buy the newspapers at the Publicis
de l'Etoile, to find out exactly how bad it had been.
We were parked in front of the Arc de Triomphe
beneath a lamppost, and since Marie had forgotten to bring her glasses, she asked me to read her,
one after the other, the reviews in the *Figaro, Au-
rore,* and so on. "Press reviews, bad news." Automatically, reading the reviews, I made an effort
to leave out any cutting remarks that referred to
her, concentrating more on the ones concerning
me. It was no good; she made me read and reread every one, and they were awful. And the more
I read, the more she laughed; for she had suddenly burst out laughing in between two abusive
remarks along the lines of "execrable dialogue
. . . hopeless acting . . . non-existent direction

. . . devoid of interest . . ." and after that she could not stop. And then of course I began laughing with her. But it was less to my credit than to hers. For after all, it was her theatre, her money, her performance as leading lady; she had more to lose than I. So that marvelous, irresistible, resounding laugh wracking the Phèdre at my side, in her beautiful Mercedes, seemed to me to presage a firm friendship—and I was not mistaken. It is unusual to make friends among theatre people on the night of a flop. It was my good fortune—and remains so—to have discovered on the occasion of that first setback one of my best friends.

My third dramatic foray was a success. I met Danielle Darrieux in *La Robe Mauve de Valentine (Valentine's Violet Gown)*, which I had written for her without knowing it. The first day of rehearsals, she came on stage and *was* Valentine; there was no need for either Jacques Robert—always a fine director—or myself to give her any hints or suggestions. To tell the truth, I was already jubilant and wasn't worried about the fate of my play. I could see stretching out before me two happy months, and as with gambling, only if you love the theatre would you be able to understand.

The magic of rehearsals, the smell of newly

cut wood that hangs over the set, the last-minute chaos, the excitement, the passion, the optimism, the despair—these have been often enough described by all and sundry, and I have nothing more to add. Let me simply say that it was autumn; in Paris the weather kept changing from sunshine to rain, but for me it always remained the same because there were only six real hours in every day, always the same hours and always in total darkness. There were armchairs in that darkness into which two or three shadows in different parts of the room would feel their way and sit down, with those pale sheets of paper that would rustle in the dark. And walking up and down on stage, regal and unreal, was my Valentine: Darrieux pursuing her way to the climax. There were breaks during which we drank a glass or two in her dressing room. And there were jolly days, when everything went well; then we would go and celebrate in a Paris that had become quite alien to us and had lost its identity, since it did not fall within the bounds of the Théâtre des Ambassadeurs. After the tension of rehearsals, we would meet complete strangers and within a few minutes would become the best of friends, though we knew that afterward they would be just as quickly and totally forgotten. Only those who had some connection with our play, our show, our achievement, were admitted to our infernal circle. We were

fanatics, sworn to martyrdom or triumph, adher-
ents of a religion no one else had ever heard of,
whose psalms we knew by heart. This made us the
most exclusive minority imaginable. Even our
husbands—Danielle Darrieux's and mine—had
been caught up in this engulfing force, and I believe they knew the play as well as we did. From
time to time, even outside the theatre, Danielle
Darrieux would talk like Valentine, think like Valentine. This amazed us all. The day of the opening I knew that the audience would like it—because it could not be otherwise, because she was
there—and indeed they did.

*Château in Sweden, And Sometimes Violins, Val-
entine's Violet Gown*—I realized that from a superb Swedish château, I had slipped down to a
well-to-do apartment in the provinces, then positively tumbled to a seedy hotel in the 14th arrondissement. I decided to climb back up the social
ladder and emigrated to St. Petersburg and the
private residence of a penniless but spendthrift
count. I wrote *Bonheur, Impair et Passe (The Wheel
of Happiness)* and took on board some very good
and fun-loving friends: Juliette Greco, Jean-Louis
Trintignant, Daniel Gélin and the very dear, very
talented and very charming Michel de Ré, who is
no longer with us. Alice Cocéa, who was, I be-

lieve, appearing on stage for the last time with this role, played mother and mother-in-law to this little group of people. As for myself, suddenly overcome with delusions of grandeur, I played director. Somehow at the end of a hazy but lively conversation I had demonstrated to I don't know which unfortunate individual that directing was a new art, completely overrated, that for the last thirty years it had been praised to the skies, but that in the past neither Molière nor Racine had concerned themselves with it. That Jean Anouilh gave proof of this with every one of his plays, brilliantly directing the actors himself. The powers ascribed to directors were excessive and unjustified, I declared, and to prove it, I was going to take on this sacrosanct responsibility myself! I convinced whomever I was talking to and, alas, myself as well. And that is how all my actors and I came to be on the stage of the Théâtre Edouard VII one lovely autumn afternoon with no other supervision and no other guidance than that which I alone provided.

I was perhaps not completely wrong in principle, but I was wrong about myself. I had forgotten, first of all, that Jean Anouilh was an authoritative person; second, he did not mumble; and third, he did not see in his actors future drinking companions. I did. Despite the talent, the sincere good will and the genuine efforts of my cast, we were soon floundering, all thanks to me. As you must know, the Théâtre Edouard VII is situated in a blind alley between the Bar du Cyros, which is quite inviting, and a Russian restaurant-bar no less charming and always open. In no time, we were living on piroshki and vodka (vodka being an excellent remedy for indecisive directors), and laughing heedlessly. I have rarely seen such chaos, so many amorous intrigues, so much giggling and tomfoolery as backstage in the Théâtre Edouard VII during those two months of rehearsals. Even now I cannot pass by that alleyway without a feeling of lightheartedness and retrospective amusement, far removed, terrible though it is to admit, from any sense whatsoever of remorse. And yet . . . I wasted my actors' time; my producers (Marie Bell, in association with Claude Génia) lost money; and I wasted the potential of a play that in fact had some charm.

As an example, let me cite, as the moment the subtlety of my direction reached its peak, the afternoon that Juliette Greco sprained her ankle tripping on a slippery rope while practicing for the annual celebrity benefit, the Gala des Artistes. Now, in the second act of my play that same evening, according to my stage directions, Juliette was to join on stage Michel de Ré, in a wheelchair, and Jean-Louis Trintignant, with his arm bandaged up and folded across his chest—both were casualties of a duel. When it became clear that she would have to remain prostrate on a sofa with her foot stuck out between the other two invalids, I didn't know what to do.

And then, on the last night of rehearsals, I happened upon one of those plainspoken onlookers who always turn up in a theatre the day before dress rehearsal—an onlooker who was not only plainspeaking but turned out to be half deaf.

"Impossible to hear anything, isn't it?" he said morosely after the final run-through. "I don't imagine they'll be able to hear any better tomorrow."

Why did I take any notice of him? It's a mystery. In any event, I stayed up all night with a sound technician and some equally dedicated electricians, installing a complete, supposedly ultramodern amplification system. The technician must have forgotten some small detail in his haste, because when we tried it out for the first time the following day, the loudspeakers began whistling so loudly when anyone opened his mouth that we stood there rooted to the spot. We should have abandoned it there and then in my opinion, but since my producers had wisely refused to have anything to do with my miraculous system and I had paid for it out of my own pocket, my actors kindly objected to the idea that I should have impoverished myself for nothing. And so the dress rehearsal took place in a weird atmosphere—it was as if the theatre were some kind of interstellar spacecraft, with sound effects reminiscent of *Star Wars*, whistlings and rumblings that sounded really very up-to-date, though a bit anachronistic for St. Petersburg in 1900. I saw our invited audience leave, one person tossing his head like a startled horse, another blocking his ears with his fingers, a third person swallowing desperately and painfully. Naturally the poor critics suffered, too, and it was another flop.

I would like to add however that, thanks to every member of the cast, this flop played for three months to reasonably satisfied audiences (the loudspeakers were, in the end, removed). And that those three months were delightful, since I considered it my duty to sustain the troops who had suffered defeat because of my negligence. In order to keep them going, I continued to join them in downing piroshki and vodka, which made us quite the most exhausted but cheerful troupe in Paris.

My number-one producer, Marie Bell, was less cheerful. She had been out of Paris during rehearsals, and therefore had not been able to intervene either in the casting or in the selection of the stage set, and she is a woman who likes to be consulted. Having come back for the final rehearsals, she kept looking at me reprovingly until the fatal dress rehearsal, when her eyes positively blazed with anger. After this spectacular preview, she summoned me to her office where she stood waiting for me behind her desk with Claude Génia, the pair of them looking like a couple of Furies.

"And are you pleased with yourself?" she asked me when I entered the room looking rather sheepish. She sounded furious (and they had been listening to the play in their office, and must have thought theirs was the only loudspeaker emitting those terrible extraterrestrial whistlings!).

"So-so," I replied prudently.

"And what do you think you're going to do next?" Marie enquired, outraged and splendid in her black sheath dress and heavy jewels.

I struck an attitude of inspiration, come what might. "As a matter of fact, I have the beginning of my next play," I said coldly. "Listen. 'What is it making that awful noise in the branches, Soames?' 'It's the wind in the trees, Milady.' "

And there I stopped. For once in her life, Marie looked nonplussed.

"And then?" she couldn't help asking.

"And then that's all," I said. "I only have the beginning. But we can use the same actors, and the same set—after the great start we've made, it won't have had time to wear out. After all, this play isn't going to . . .''

At that point, I made a quick exit, before gentle Marie could hurl a glass at me.

As it happened, two years later the curtain of the Gymnase rose upon the dress rehearsal of a play in which an English lady downstage is heard to say: "What is it making that awful noise in the branches, Soames?" "It's the wind in the trees, milady." Which just goes to show that as liars would have it, "When you have the first two lines of dialogue, you already have the rest of the play." The play in question was called *Le Cheval Evanoui (The Vanished Horse)*, and it went very well. It was followed by several others that suffered various fates, but I won't go into detail about them now, as that would be too tedious. Let me simply say that the most spectacular flop of my career was that of my last play, *Il Fait Beau Jour et Nuit (Sunshine Day and Night)*.

As I was leaving the house wearing evening dress, my dog followed me to the door, wagging its tail, and before I could shut it in behind me, it was suddenly sick all over my gown. I raced to get changed and, since I was late, I was still racing when two traffic police stopped me on the road for a good half hour. I eventually arrived, only to learn that in my absence a cable had broken on

107

the elevator at the Comédie des Champs-Elysées
and the car, carrying a party of Parisian high society, had plunged thirty-five feet, throwing my
guests all over the place, perhaps causing them
no physical damage but certainly impairing their
good humor. During the performance, a woman
fainted—the heat was partly responsible—and
several well-known people fell asleep. Eight heroic individuals came backstage to see me after
the performance, and the press was unanimous
in retracting all previous testimonies to my talent
as a playwright.

   As always in such situations, I whistled gaily
for the next fortnight at least; a failure in the theatre is, for me anyway, much more stimulating
than a success. For if you have a success, what
can you do but lower your eyes, simper, act coy,
and point to the cast and director and say: "It's got
nothing to do with me, it's all due to them . . .
No, no, you're too kind . . . I'm delighted you
liked it . . ." and so forth. On the other hand,
when it's a flop, you first of all have to remind the
cast, in tears all around you, that it's not the end
of the world, that things are much worse in Chad,
and this spell in purgatory that we have been living for the past two months has not after all led
to hell. And then when it comes to dealing with
the others, those spurious friends who enjoy your
discomfiture—and there are, alas, always a cer-

tain number of these, as Parisians know all too well—it is absolutely imperative to put a good face on it. The rules of the theatre are like those of chemin de fer, of the roulette wheel. Smile, whistle and say, "Ah well, it was pretty bad, wasn't it? Never mind, these things happen. And, after all, worse things happen." By dint of affecting insouciance, it becomes genuine. Three months' exertion and excitement, three months' mental effort and running here and there—three months' work, in fact—reduced to nothing in an hour-and-a-half's performance: there's something heroic about it, something mad, unjust, romantic. And because of this something, I could no more give up the theatre than I could the casino—whatever happens.

Rudolf Nureyev

We were to meet Rudolf Nureyev in Amsterdam, a place I knew no better than I knew Rudolf Nureyev. It was the beginning of March. The rain was bucketing down on this peaceful town and its canals. And I wondered anxiously what we were going to find to talk about, this famous stranger and I. I admired him certainly, but it was a benighted admiration, not the enlightened kind of a balletomane who would be able to talk about the subject. I knew nothing about dance, so my admiration was for the beauty of the man himself, and the beauty I had recognized in his performance on stage in Paris. I had seen him come running into the spotlights, I had seen him leap with triumphant energy, and I had realized somewhere within me that his leaps, his steps were more beautiful, more energetic, more brilliant than those of other dancers.

Some time after, our paths had crossed one night on the nightclub circuit. A winged pedestrian, quick, relaxed, with a lupine face and a Russian laugh, he had at that time numbered among that great family of nightbirds. It had been easy to exchange one or two friendly but meaningless pleasantries of the kind strangers in the night are familiar with. But in Amsterdam, a quiet town turned in on itself, in the warmth and good order of a bourgeois restaurant, I was for a moment virtually incapable of establishing any kind of rapport with this young forty-year-old.

And yet he was cheerful, he laughed, he was as relaxed and friendly as he was reputed not to be, and I was horrified by the thought that he was having to make an effort, when it ought to have been up to me to do so. Patrons of the restaurant came over to our table to ask him for his autograph, and with a sarcastic laugh he obligingly gave them his signature, passing some acid remark as he did so, so that it momentarily crossed my mind, and the thought wearied me, that he might be bitter.

A few taxi rides later, after a few vain attempts to catch up with a night on the town such as Amsterdam cannot provide, or at least could not provide us with that night, we ended up at two o'clock in the morning sitting in armchairs in our hotel lounge, feeling tired and a little disappointed, although, as far as I was concerned, I couldn't tell whether it was disappointment in him or in myself. And then I asked him, I think, whether he liked people, life, his life, and he leaned forward to reply, his ironic indifferent face transformed into that of an ingenuous child, anxious to make himself understood, and to tell the truth. Sensitive, intelligent and disarmed, his face asked, indeed required that all questions be put to him.

We stayed in Amsterdam for three days, lunching and dining with Nureyev, and in all the time we tagged along with him, he never once departed from a casual easy graciousness which, given the draconian timetable this favored child had to observe, was nothing less than the epitome of courtesy. I no longer remember exactly what questions I asked him, nor his replies. In any case, my questions were probably very vague; but I am quite certain that the uncommon exactitude of the replies reflected a great sincerity. One word kept springing to his lips: the verb "fulfill." "I want to fulfill my life," he would say. And in order to "fulfill his life," there had been, there was, and there would always be dance, his Art. He spoke of his art with the kind of anxious respect primitives have for their totems.

At the age of six, Nureyev had been to see a performance of *Swan Lake* in the far reaches of his native Siberia, and he decided there and then to be a dancer. For eleven years he knew, without ever once being able to prove it to himself, that he would be a dancer. In his hometown there was no dancing class of any kind, and traditional folk dances gave him his only opportunity to perform in public. Then his talent was recognized, he was discovered, and went to Leningrad or Moscow—I don't remember which—and in two or three years, starting from scratch, he had to learn the strict constraints and laws, the uncompromising discipline of the art that was his passion.

For three years he took no rest, he had no time to sit down, go to bed, sleep, allow his muscles to relax, acquire the line and assume the fineness, the elegant slimness of those of his fellow dancers. Nureyev's legs—his calves and thighs—are very powerful, unusually well developed for a man of his stature. They create an impression of incredible vigor, and suggest an earthly dimension in this body whose torso, arms and neck are so light, so skyward-reaching.

At the end of these three years, he was acknowledged as the best dancer in all Russia, supreme, unique. But his fellow dancers who had gone traveling in far-off Europe had returned with amateurishly shot 8mm films with jumpy images, on which they had nevertheless recorded what others abroad were doing, their innovations—all the things which he, the very best, would never know, and which in his conscience and soul prevented him from feeling that he was really and truly the best.

It wasn't freedom or luxury or a good time or distinctions that Nureyev dreamed of when he boarded the plane which would take him far away from Moscow forever, away from his homeland, his family; his dreams were of Balanchine, Balanchine's art, its inventiveness and its boldness. And that is why, I believe, that even now, when you talk to him about his mother and his sisters, whom he has not set eyes on for eighteen years, whom he has only been able to speak to over the phone; why even now, although his expression becomes impenetrable and he falls silent at the mere idea of it, he never for a single instant regrets having left. He is almost a caricature, the virtual embodiment of the romantic but well-worn cliché that seems so pretentious, according to which a man's only homeland, his only family, is his art. Since his arrival in Paris, for the past eighteen years he has not ceased to seek out, to experiment, to develop and create for himself all the possibilities to which music gives his body access. He dances everywhere, and superbly, in many familiar and acclaimed ballets, but he does so in order to be able to introduce new ballets, to bring to people a modern art that is still vital and often difficult, one that he alone, perhaps, is capable of imposing on a public as conservative as it is snobbish.

He travels all over the world, visiting one town after another. He is a man who lives in airplanes and hotels, and on trains; he is a man who never stops, and his private life, like his body, obeys a rhythm which he dictates. He has many friends and yet not one friend, many lovers and yet not one love, he is often alone but never lonesome, because the only luggage he never lets out of his sight, a case full of cassettes, accompanies him everywhere. In the evening in New York, Nureyev comes home to a hotel room much like the one in Berlin he left the day before, and the one which awaits him tomorrow in London. He kicks off his shoes, lies down on the bed, listens to the noise of the city, reaches out and presses a button: music by Mahler or Tchaikovsky wells up and this room becomes the room where he spent his childhood, his youth, and where he will spend his life to come; it becomes the warm familiar cradle of his lone reveries.

People may well applaud him the next day—and he likes applause and needs it; this he admits without shame or apology. People may well hail his performance as miraculous, or decry it as a disappointment. They may proclaim him the greatest dancer ever, or deny that he is that any longer. They may well talk in hushed tones of his escapades, of the scandals with which he has been associated, and of his standoffishness—Nureyev couldn't care less. Reality for him is not this avid and loyal following and the gossip it thrives on; it is not the huge unseeing and unhearing planes constantly crossing immense oceans, or the hotel rooms indistinguishable one from the other, or even the beds onto which he throws down kilos of fatigue and mingled sweat and makeup (his bed is the best, the most faithful and most tender of lovers, he says). Reality for him is the three hours or six hours which await him every afternoon in one of the remorselessly identical studios situated in the heart of every town.

One afternoon in Amsterdam we went to watch him in rehearsal. The studio was a watery-green and brown and looked bleak and dirty, with tarnished mirrors and a squeaky wooden floor—a studio just like any other. Over his leotard he wore tired woolen leggings with holes in them. A record player was hesitantly scratching out a piece of music by Bach. He stopped when he saw us enter, just long enough to say something funny and mop up the sweat. I watched him dry his neck, his chest and his face with rather rough and ready gestures that were strangely detached, just as a stable boy might groom his horse. Then he put the needle back to the beginning of the record and, having removed his wristbands and leggings, he went and stood in the middle of the room, still smiling. The music started and he stopped smiling. He took up his position with arms outstretched, and studied himself in the mirror. I had never seen anyone examine himself in that way before. People look at themselves in a mirror with fear, complacency, embarrassment, and usually rather timidly, but they never look at themselves with the eyes of a stranger. Nureyev observed his body, his head, the movements of his neck with an objectivity, a well-disposed coldness that were completely new to me. He reached out, projecting his body forward, performed a perfect arabesque, landed with one knee on the ground, his arms magnificently poised. This movement he accomplished with a feline grace and speed, and in the mirror was a perfect reflection of virility and gracefulness combined in a single body. And throughout the rehearsal, while his body was visibly influenced by the music and became infused with it, while he danced faster and faster and leaped higher and higher, seemingly carried away by gods totally unknown to the rest of us, in introspective reverie, he continued to watch himself in exactly the same way, like a master looking at his servant, or a servant his master; and the look in his eye was indefinable, demanding and sometimes almost tender.

He returned to the beginning of the same piece two or three times, and each time was different and beautiful in a different way. Then the music stopped; he finally brought it to an end with one of those consummately imperious gestures that belong to people replete with something that lies beyond everyday life. He came over to us, smiling, and with the same distracted gestures toweled dry the soaking-wet, trembling, breathless instrument which served him as a body. I began to have an inkling of what he meant by the word "fulfill."

After that, of course, we had Nureyev leaping about on the quaysides in Amsterdam, Nureyev eternally young, showing how charming he could be, then how demanding; sometimes warm as a brother, sometimes withdrawn and impatient as a stranger in hostile territory. He has charm, generosity, sensitivity and imagination to spare, and as a result he has a hundred different faces, and probably a thousand different psychological profiles.

Naturally I don't imagine that I have understood very much about this genius of a creature who is Nureyev. But if I had to find a way to describe the man, or to put it more precisely, come up with an image that would capture him symbolically, as I see him, I could find none better than this: that of a half-naked man in his leotard, alone and handsome, raised on tiptoe, gazing into a tarnished mirror, with mistrustful and wondering eyes, on the reflection of his art.

Saint-Tropez

It is mid-June. I am sitting on the terrace of the
Hotel de la Ponche, in Saint-Tropez, at six o'clock
in the evening. Though it is very nearly summer,
overhead is a lead-gray sky shot with not the
slightest trace of pink.

I have both feet up on a chair to avoid the
puddles. A book lies in my lap. I have been trying
in vain to read the same page for the past hour.
People walk by before my eyes wearing that ridiculous getup a rainy summer requires—a combi-
nation of a pair of shorts and a parka, an expres-

sion on their faces of children unjustly punished. On the table to my right, an ice cube is almost melted in a glass of lemonade that remains warm, as warm as the rain which has just started to fall again and which drips onto my hair, my cheek and finally forces me to get up and go inside.

A week ago in Paris I had gotten out of bed one fine morning—or rather, one morning like any other: rain and more rain without a break, people on the streets looking anxious, dejected and alarmed, the city looking haggard and no sign of the sky. That morning I took flight—as is my custom—and headed for the sea and Saint-Tropez. But for the first time in my life, the clouds did not break up at Lyons, disperse at Valence and fade away once we reached the Maures. For the first time in my life, I arrived to find the same gray sky over the bay as in the city, to see the same iron-gray reflections in the waters of the Mediterranean as upon the Seine. It had rained all the way there, and it was raining still. There had been no spring; there would be no summer; fear, sadness and depression had been my driving companions for six hundred miles on this trail of a sun in eclipse.

And yet it is June, and only 1980. Another twenty years before that fateful year 2000, which a succession of Cassandras have prophesied we will never see, having fallen victim to our applied

sciences and spiritual ignorance. It is quite possible that, one mistake leading to another, madness outstripping madness, some all-powerful
Chosen One or some demented nonentity might
lay waste this beautiful planet and set it ablaze.
We might well die at a stroke, senselessly incin-
erated, and not even long afterwards would anyone know why or how, or even who was responsible . . .

And yet I am about to tell you the tragicomic story
of my past and no doubt future sentimental at-
tachment to the peaceful little town of Saint-
Tropez, in the Var. I will tell the story in several
acts, several tableaux—how many I cannot say
right from the start, memory being just as giddy
and unpredictable as the imagination. I cannot
vouch for the total objectivity or the total accu-
racy of the facts which follow; I can vouch only for
my sincerity of this moment. And that's already
something, given the town in question, more of a
village really, a place that still inspires in those who
love it, whatever their age, an obsessiveness about
the past and extravagant memories that are always impressive for their frantic gaiety or frantic
melancholy. And in both cases for their emotive-
ness. Saint-Tropez is a town, a village that trig-
gers off a daydream, a craziness that is either

pleasant or not—in any case something which cannot be triggered off in the same way, instantly and in every single person, by any other place in the world. Here then is my own personal comedy.

ACT I

The action takes place in 1954 or '55. The setting is a small port one pale blue morning. It is spring. A convertible, an old Jaguar X440, covered in dust, has just parked along the quayside. At the wheel is a tousle-haired young man (my brother) and by his side a tousle-haired young girl (myself). Our two heroes are red-eyed, and blink in the harsh light. They have driven down on National Highway 7, a long roadway full of bends and in bad condition that used to pass through urban areas, linger in villages, stop outside cafes. Users of the road grew accustomed to doing as they pleased when traveling on this highway. They would stop wherever they liked, talk to the waiters—who were not yet nickel-plated or coin-operated—and even had the gall to stop on the grass beneath a tree far from any so-called "rest areas." It even happened that cars that met along these potholed, two-way roads did so head-on. The only attraction of these dangerous roads: there were no tolls.

Having miraculously survived this highway of

another age, of a kind impossible to imagine today, the two young people get out of their car and make their way toward the one and only real estate agency. Likewise later they will celebrate their arrival in the port's only bar, called L'Escale and run by old lady Mado—a dark-roomed, provincial cafe that smells of wood, insecticide and lemonade. And likewise too, that afternoon, they will trade in their Parisian garb for unbleached cottons and rope espadrilles in the only shop in town, a shop called Vachon that is run by a friendly woman and her family (one of the town's five families, as one might say one of the two hundred families of France). In this first act and in a rapid succession of tableaux, our two characters visit eight or nine houses, all empty, all beautiful, all perched precariously on rocks that are themselves balanced on the only stable element in the village: the smooth blue waters of its shore. They choose the largest villa, the one nearest La Ponche (which means "fishing port" in the local dialect) and they move in.

By themselves at first, they are soon joined by pale-skinned friends, casualties of city life, heroic friends whose turn it is now to pile out of their cars, having also braved the vicissitudes and dangers of National Highway 7. These bewildered Parisians take a seat in the bar in La Ponche, and are able at last to rest their weary eyes (theirs a monumental weariness such as only a twenty-year-old knows), looking now to the left at the old ladies of the neighborhood knitting in concert (in this particular case a concert of voices and sublime accents); now to the right, at the blue-green coast of Sainte-Maxime in the distance and the splashes of white that are its houses; now at the fishing boats and their weather-bleached sails as they either set out for the catch of the bay ("the gilt-head bream of the blue deep, those fish of gold, those fish that sing . . ." that Rimbaud spoke of), or return at dawn on a colorless sea to the dull, rhythmic vibration of their two-stroke engines. This will be the only summer and the only tableau in my Saint-Tropez comedy when all you can see to the left are women peacefully knitting, and all you can see to the right are seamen idling. This will be the only summer when you will see people working. And thus a calm reigning over the village.

ACT II

It is when we come to Act II that we will see, in contrast, holidays, leisure pursuits and lotus-eating idleness in all their remorseless activity take over to right and left of the house. To the left we will see wild and disorderly groups of urban bathing beauties as they rush from street stall to street stall in search of a swimsuit, and to the right, speedboats and the rowdy screaming and shouting of young people who roar off in unruly disarray—all for the feeble purpose of lying on the sand five hundred yards farther down the beach. That is Saint-Tropez's greatest virtue and its greatest fault; it reverses roles and robs words of their former meaning. I will come back to this . . .

All of which goes to say that there was only one year in that house in La Ponche that seemed normal to my friends and to myself: the year when Saint-Tropez was ours (of course), the year we were the only ones to use and abuse the sea, the sand, the solitude and beauty, the only ones to use and abuse the kindness and stunned patience of its inhabitants; the only ones to hoot our horns at dawn in the narrow streets; to behave like cheeky hooligans with two policemen, making them laugh, and when they called us *fada* (the local Provençal word for "cracked in the head,") it didn't yet seem a cheap and nasty aping of Marcel Pagnol (as it did the second year, before dropping from the vocabulary).

Things moved quickly in the second act, the second tableau. Already my memory is muddled . . . Vadim came and made *And God Created Woman* in the port, or finished making it. Brigitte Bardot bought La Madrague and fell for Jean-Louis

Trintignant. Alexandre Astruc decided to make a brilliant film with my collaboration. Michel Magne wrote symphonies for bassoon and horn on the old out-of-tune organ in our big house, and in the Place de la Ponche, Monsieur and Madame Barbier put a few tables outside, adding to the counter and the eight stools that constituted the Bar des Pêcheurs (today it has become the Hôtel de la Ponche, but the spirit of Albert still presides, as does the ingenuous humor of his wife). All these creative—and, it must be said, unbridled—young people had found their way to the house in La Ponche by the end of summer. The film director Vadim came with his camera and his heart weary from all the filming. The actor Christian Marquand sat down with his huge bulk and the casualness of a dissipated man, with his laugh and his schoolboy excitement. The film was out quickly in a dozen picture houses. In Paris it "knocked them dead" at once, as it was to do to us the following year.

ACT III

And so the sun of glory (not to mention the other one above, that round jaunty star we call the Sun), that piercing and corrupt sun of glory weighed heavily over Saint-Tropez, now suddenly the metropolis of illicit pleasures. In fact, it was not until 1960 that the word "pleasure" was no longer automatically paired with the word "illicit" and was replaced ipso facto by the word "mandatory." French humanoids, until then quite unaware of amorality, debauchery and the most basic laws of sexuality—either in terms of the scantiness of bathing suits or simply in terms of broad-mindedness (and sometimes unaware that the two terms need not necessarily be yoked together)— like pilgrims to Mecca or Canossa, now beat a path to Saint-Tropez, headed for so-called "Fun" with a capital F, on the trail of the docile black sheep that we had become, we film directors, musicians, actors, producers and writers, we the temporary, bronzed archetypes of *Paris-Match* and *France-Dimanche*.

We, the two-legged exemplars, begin to smile a sickly smile beneath our suntans. We too have to stand in line at Vachon, so we go off in a huff to Choses or Mic Mac, two rival stores that have dared to set up shop in the port. And at Tahiti's we too have to pay more than cost price for crayfish that Felix, the happy proprietor, no longer catches himself. Saint-Tropez still belongs to us, of course; and the shopkeepers and landlords who've profitably exploited the town's attractions still play the part of parasites—"our" parasites, more or less loyal and more or less expensive, naturally, but in any case still grateful for the manna we have brought them, like young royal magi. But we are no longer alone on the beaches. Golden days and nights without sleep, fits of laughter in the dusk, chases down the alleyways, love affairs without sequels and indiscretions without consequences are no longer ours alone to enjoy. As for the frenzied debauchery of which we are accused: we see others indulge in it, but with no grace or ingenuity, of course.

It is the frenzied debauchery of money that fast takes over, ostentatious and remorseless. Of course success and achievement retain their allure and are still won through something other than greed, or dexterity, or opportunism; of course when Felix, Roger and François, who are the same age as we are and don't have a penny between them, open L'Esquinade and make it into as successful a nightspot as Tabarin or Tabou, their success is still chancy and gratifying because all three of them are a little mad, dead broke, irresponsible and charming. They will probably number among the last of the kind of bartender who is closer to F. Scott Fitzgerald than to James Bond.

Yes, but . . . In only two years money's everywhere: it may try to disguise itself, stripping down to the waist and running with the wind in the sails of a racing boat or behind the wheel of a roaring Ferrari, acting depraved, sporty, arty or

even ecologically minded; it's no use, money remains detectable nonetheless. It has struck at the
heart of the town. It is hidden beneath the placid
statue of Admiral Suffren, the town patron; it keeps
watch over everything, and holds everything in its
power. Already the policemen have given up saying "*fada*," already you can't buy fish at dawn
straight from the holds of the fishing boats anymore, already no one but a Texan bothers sailors
unwise enough to be sitting in the port with questions like "And what kind of weather are we in for
tomorrow, skipper?" or "What's your poison then,
mate?" Already some of us, sitting around together in the evening, have begun talking of Normandy . . .

ACT IV
Tableaux 1, 2, 3, 4

Things went from bad to worse during the winter—one winter, or two, who can tell? . . . Certain staunch Saint-Tropezians who'd become
people of note by issuing bills, and certain out-
siders now considered a credit to the community
because they honored their credit, had put a stop
to what little easygoing liberality still remained in
town. No one knows the how or the when or the
why of it, the sweet, prototypal bipeds having been

involved in the vagaries of their emotional lives, or their careers, or their moods, and having as a result missed out on one or perhaps two of those divine summers (which still seem so in memory even now) . . . And yet it's clear. You can see it yourself. You can hear it in the tone of voice of some of the local youngsters on the corner whose prospects are no longer so uncertain, whose tone of voice no longer carries the least suggestion of gratitude—which none of the bipeds expected anyway, I'm sure—but neither does it convey an edge of complicity, in which many bipeds believed so foolishly and the absence of which so profoundly disconcerts them in private. *Que sont mes amis devenus? (What has become of my friends?)* "They've become rich," we answer the troubadour Rutebeuf, disconcerted as we are by the fifty shirt shops, twenty hotels, forty bistros, ten nightclubs, twelve real estate agencies, and five antique shops that have replaced Mado, L'Agence du Port, Vachon and Leï Mouscardins on my right, L'Auberge des Maures on my left (two restaurants I did not mention at the beginning of this tragicomedy, since Colette used to dine there fifty years ago, nor did I mention the church, and the town hall) . . .

In short, in Saint-Tropez today no longer do you go from pleasure to pleasure, from secret rendezvous to secret rendezvous, from one corner of the beach to another corner, one bedroom to another. Instead you go from a dinner party at X's house to a dinner party at Y's; you go from Club Number One to Club Number Two; at night you go from one circle of friends to another, and during the day, from one purchase to another. No one is happy hunter or willing victim; instead you go from clique to clique and story to story. It's like some Greek tragedy, with Euripides as man-about-town inspired by Feydeau as sociologist: no love affair exists unless it's talked about, no beach exists unless you have to pay to sit on it, no desire exists unless you can put a price on it. Saint-Tropez is now a sort of prelude to Reno, Nevada: couples go to Saint-Tropez to make the break, in other words to do publicly, in a manner calculated to hurt their partner, what they would do on the sly in Paris. Betrayals and breakups are sooner flaunted than is happiness. It's no longer laughter that rules in the night, or pleasure, or curiosity; it is a kind of permanent display—usually false—of gaiety, pleasure, curiosity, a mere show that is gradually spreading over a society as bourgeois, as rigid, as gossip-mongering and provincial as any town can be, or could be, were its denizens to have only rights and no more responsibilities. And certainly no proper upbringing: people throw Coke bottles onto the beach and hundred-franc notes at the waiters' feet, they throw

glasses from their balconies—and all these mis-
siles represent the proprieties they have thrown to
the wind. Germans, Americans, Italians and others think they're buying themselves enchantment
as they pour marks, dollars, and lire onto the blue
carpet of the Mediterranean, a Mediterranean in
which fish die from all the gasoline, where the
beaches are filthy by the first day of spring, and
where you have to take a box of Band-Aids with
you if you walk barefoot on the sand at night.

A bleak tableau, of course, but that's how the
bipeds—and I was one—see it, bipeds who, like
me, have abandoned the pink and golden town
that was once theirs. Bipeds who (like me at this
moment) haven't a good word to say about the
Saint-Tropez they loved so well; or who draw from
their memories, like rabbits out of a hat, the
sparkling, nostalgic recollections of youth—their
own youth—which they consider different from and
clearly superior to the youth of those who followed. The conflict between generations of tourists that now rages in this village of discord has
its comic side. As when in the course of certain
epic recitals, heard a thousand times before, the
memory crops up of some old dandy, once a tar-
get for our childish cruelty, and more than one of
our sarcastic forty-year-old bipeds can be seen to
fuss with his English scarf, tucking it into the duck
shirt that cost him a fortune at Saks in New York,

as he draws himself up and displays all the wrinkles and tics that his memory saw in someone else just a moment before. Or the way women of forty or fifty look upon "all those young chippies parading their wares . . . they've no class . . . they don't know what a good time is . . . the poor things . . . they don't know how to enjoy themselves any more . . . ," wondering, with all their own experience, whether the young ones enjoy making love—this maternal anxiety is not lacking in irony.

My story could well end on the same note—Act IV, Scene 5, 1999: our gray-haired, pot-bellied bipeds look on sardonically as their forty-year-old offspring criticize their own twenty-year-old children, remarking derisively, "Yes, oh yes, young people today know how to have a good time, and they're not at all frigid" (this said with the sheer malice of old age, of course).

But this would be a false and sadly sordid ending to what was, is and will remain Saint-Tropez. Time passes but memory holds fast, thank God. Just as, two thousand years ago, a forty-year-old Roman came in his chariot as far as Ostia and bemoaned his fate on the beach, or a hundred miles or so from there a Greek woman lamented the infidelity of her husband, so now we stand at the blue-waters' edge bewailing our mortality and the transience of youth. Did it occur to that Roman or that Greek that the sea would continue to lap the warm sands into which the soles of their feet were sinking, and that the sun would continue to rise and set lengthening the shadows of trees and houses on the earth's surface even when their eyes no longer beheld it, even when they no longer breathed in and out in time with the beating of their hearts? And did not the sea, the sun, the smell of pine, salt and iodine inspire in them a delicious pleasure quite incompatible with the notion that all this would survive them?

Today the forty-year-old who arrives in an Aston Martin, or by bus, or in a camper and pitches himself beside the blue waterfront with the same exhilaration as gold diggers in the Klondike around their mines—he and the tourists from all over the world suffer from the same wonderful ailment: admiration. Saint-Tropez is beautiful, stunningly beautiful. It has an indestructible beauty—especially for us, the bipeds, the now dispossessed proprietors who used to drive down National Highway 7—as we realize, with surprise and almost ungrudging pleasure, when we return during the cease-fires, in spring, autumn or winter.

There are above all the winds, the three or four winds that catch the isthmus and sweep over it, sprucing it up, dispersing an air so light and mad and gay that inside two days you feel a different person; it's a real tonic. There's the peaceful yellow sun, a pleasant sun that often shines when it's raining in Cannes and in Monte Carlo. There's the red-hued coastline with its intricate inlets and its sudden smooth beaches, a coastline which is like some of Racine's tragedies, where first you're caught up treading dialogue, then released into the expanse of a soliloquy. There's "the crazed sea that cracks its cups at the brim," as Cocteau put it, where more than anywhere else it is foamy, arresting and cool. There's the countryside, the real countryside hidden behind Saint-Tropez, which is green, unlike the rest of the Maures with its bare, rocky landscape, impoverished and sunbaked. For immediately beyond the beach in Saint-Tropez there are fields, bright green grass, woods, cork oaks, hills like those in the Île-de-France, water, trees, the smell of rotting wood in autumn and of mushrooms. And there are paths, beyond Pampelonne, that you can walk along without knowing where they lead.

But whether seen from the sea or from above, from the citadel where no one ever goes, Saint-Tropez shows off its narrow pointed houses, houses that sometimes lurch this way and that but are always heartwarming; its yellow, red and blue or gray houses, battened upon by sun and wind, with their thousand-petaled tiled roofs in faded pink, so gentle on the eye, gathered closely round an eccentric bell tower that tolls the quarter hour at any old time, though no one takes any notice. Of course, there's a bit of washing hung out to dry, just as in Italy, and a few terraces too well cared for, as are a few green plants that serve no purpose. But the walls of the houses are made of stones solidly piled one on top of the other, and no matter how many layers of plaster are applied, at whatever price, over the old, this fact cannot be concealed.

All the houses bask in the sunshine during the day, like cats or overfed dogs. They have trusting faces, even if their doors and windows are narrow, and their bellies are round. The houses like to watch you pass by at night. They have a door that bangs, that opens to draw you nearer, and a window that always has a light shining in it, to let you know where you are. The little streets cross one another higgledy-piggledy and sort themselves out at the square, where a twisted tree holds pride of place. The alleyways ring with the cries of corsairs or revelers and, to us, with our own cries of twenty years ago. You can walk for hours in Saint-Tropez, day and night. From the Place des Lices to the port; from one bistro to another; or later on, from one bakery that opens at dawn to another; from a white sea to a sea that turns gradually blue beneath the little cemetery . . . the little cemetery where everyone would like to be buried one day, able to see the boats going past, and so that the sun could warm one's unhinged bones.

ACT V

Summer 1980. The end. The curtain has fallen on a tragicomedy about Saint-Tropez. I have dozed for forty-five minutes, dreamed through twenty-five years. I awakened in a darkened room and immediately closed my eyes again, instinctively straining for a sound I couldn't hear, and which I almost missed. I finally realized that it was no longer raining and that the sharp-edged streak of light on the wall opposite me was a ray cast by that celebrated star we call the Sun. I got out of bed and opened the shutters, and the sea and the sky threw in my face a familiar blueness, a familiar pink, a familiar happiness. Equally familiar were the sunbeams that cut through all this at a single stroke, outlining these pastel colors in black, tracing with everlasting voluptuousness the ridges of the roofs, the curve of the bay, the tips of the masts. It is now 1980 and I can't say whether we will reach the year 2000 without some unseeing, dogged aircraft, its crew deaf to all orders to return to base (or some mindless monstrous rocket,

like a pitiless dinosaur from primeval times) coming for us, carrying in its belly a death that will be
a flash of light and dust.

Not that it matters terribly. The sun is here in
the palm of my hand and without thinking I hold
out my palm toward it, but do not close my hand
over it. One should no more try to keep a hold on
the sun and life than one should on time and love.
I go downstairs to people who are laughing and
forgetting, people who are ready to set off elsewhere, no matter where exactly, but somewhere
that resembles this place, or that would strive to
resemble it and never quite succeed.

Love Letter to
Jean-Paul Sartre

Cher Monsieur

I write to you as "cher monsieur" with the childishly simple dictionary definition of the word in mind—"any male person." I'm certainly not going to address you as "cher Jean-Paul Sartre"—that sounds too journalistic. "Cher Maître" evokes everything you abhor; "cher confrère" lacks all finesse. I have wanted to write this letter to you for many years—nearly thirty years, in fact; ever since I first began to read your work, and in the last ten or twelve years especially, when the expression of admiration, being so ridiculed, has become so rare that one is almost happy to be thought ridiculous. Perhaps I am old enough now—or have rediscovered enough of my youth—not to worry anymore what people may think. You yourself, with superb aplomb, have never let that bother you.

I wanted you to receive this letter on June 21, a red-letter day for France, since it marks the birth, at intervals of several years, of you, of me, and more recently of Michel Platini, three fine people whether wildly celebrated or just as senselessly trampled underfoot—in your case and mine, only figuratively speaking, thank God—attracting lavish praise or excessive criticism for reasons none of us understands. But the summers are brief, busy, and soon over. In the end I gave up the idea of "an anniversary ode," and yet I still felt I had to tell you what I am now going to say, which will explain what's behind such a sentimental title.

It was in 1950 that I really began to read, and I read everything. Since then, God (or Literature) knows how many writers I have loved and admired, especially contemporary writers, from France and elsewhere. Since then, I have got to know some of them, and I have followed the careers of others. While there are many I still admire as writers, you are the only one I continue to admire as a man. Everything you promised me when I was fifteen—an age of intelligence and high-mindedness, an age when one is without well-defined ambitions and therefore uncompromising—all these promises you have kept. You have written the most intelligent, most honest books of your generation. You have also written the most explosively talented work in all French literature—The Words. At the same time, you have always leaped into the fray to defend the weak and the oppressed; you have had faith in people and causes and in truths. You have sometimes made mistakes—all of us do—but, unlike the rest of us, you have always admitted your mistakes. You have consistently rejected any idea of distinction or material benefits for your achievement. You refused the supposed honor of the Nobel Prize when you had nothing. You were knocked down three times by terrorist bombs at the time of the war in Algeria, left homeless on the streets without batting an eyelid. You have obliged theatre directors to cast women you loved in parts to which they were not necessarily suited, thereby demonstrating magnificently that, for you, love could indeed be the "brilliant lament of glory." In short, you have loved, written, shared, given everything you had to give that was of real importance—and at the same time refused everything offered to you that merely presumed to be so. You have been as much a man as a writer; you have never claimed that the talent of the writer could justify the failings of the man, nor that the joy of lone creativity gave you leave to scorn or neglect either those close to you, or anyone else. You have not even countenanced the notion that mistakes are redeemed when made with talent and in good faith. In fact, you have never sought refuge behind the writer's well-known frailty, that double-edged weapon that is his talent. You have never played Narcissus, although it is one of only three roles writers of our age are allowed—along with that of Humble Master and Superior Manservant. Far from it. Rather than savoring the pleasure and enjoying the histrionics of impaling yourself on this supposedly double-edged weapon, as so many writers do, you have claimed that it was light in your hand, that it was effective, quick, and that you loved it. You have made use of it, putting it at the disposal of those whom you regard as the real victims, those who cannot write, nor give account of themselves, those who cannot fight, and sometimes do not even know their grievance.

You have not clamored for justice because you do not wish to make judgments. You spoke not of honor because you have no wish to be honored. You would not even call for generosity, not realizing that you yourself have always been the very soul of generosity. And yet you remain the only man of justice, honor and generosity of our time. You have worked ceaselessly, giving everything to others, living neither in luxury nor austerity, recognizing no taboos, and celebrating only—and with great exuberance—the act of writing. Making love and offering love, a seducer always ready to be seduced, you have far outstripped all your friends with your vitality, intelligence and brilliance, but are always ready to go back and meet them so that they should not be discouraged by your superiority. You have often preferred to be used and duped rather than to remain indifferent, and often to be disappointed rather than to deny hope. What an exemplary life for a man who never sought to set an example!

Now that you have lost your sight and, it is said, are no longer able to write, you must surely sometimes be as unhappy as anyone can be. Perhaps it would at least please you to know that wherever I have traveled over the past twenty years—in Japan, America, Norway, in the provinces or in Paris—I have heard men and women of all ages speak of you with the same kind of admiration, trust and gratitude that I wish to express in this letter.

This century has proved to be crazed, inhuman, rotten. You have been, and have remained,

intelligent, tenderhearted and incorruptible. For
this you deserve our thanks.

I wrote this letter in 1980 and had it published in
L'Egoiste, Nicole Wisnieck's fine, unpredictable
magazine. Naturally, I asked Sartre's permission
first, via an intermediary. It was nearly twenty years
since we had last met—and even then our meet-
ings had consisted only of a few meals together,
with Simone de Beauvoir and my first husband,
and they were rather strained occasions; a few
comical afternoon encounters in deliciously disreputable places where Sartre and I pretended not
to recognize each other; and a luncheon with a
charming businessman who was slightly besotted
with me and who invited Sartre to run a left-wing
review which he would be very happy to finance,
but when this same businessman went off between the cheese course and the coffee, to go and
change his parking disc, Sartre broke into wild
laughter of mingled amusement and despair. In
any case, de Gaulle was on the way up and that
was the end of that unlikely project.

After these few brief contacts with each other,
Sartre and I had not met for twenty years; and all
that time I had wanted to tell him how much I owed
him.

So Sartre, already blind, had this letter read

to him and asked to see me; he invited me to dine with him, just the two of us. I went to fetch him in the Boulevard Edgar-Quinet—I never pass by there now without feeling a pang of grief. We went to La Closerie des Lilas. I held him by the hand to prevent him from falling, and I was so intimidated I could not speak without stammering. I think we made the oddest pair in French literary history, and the maîtres d'hôtel fluttered about us like frighted crows.

That was one year before his death. It was the first of a long series of dinners, but I knew nothing of that at the time. I thought he had invited me out of kindness, and I also thought that I would die before him.

After that we dined together nearly every ten days. I would go and collect him. He would be waiting for me in the hall, wearing his duffel coat, and we would scuttle away like a pair of thieves, no matter who else might be there. I must confess that, contrary to what those close to him have said, and what they remember of his last months, I was never horrified or shocked by the way he ate. Of course, it was all a bit hit-or-miss, but that was because he was blind, not because he was senile. I take great exception to those who have bewailed these meals, either in articles or books, expressing distress or scorn. They should have closed their eyes if their eyes were so easily offended, and listened to him speak; listened to that light-hearted, courageous, strong voice, and appreci-ated the freedom that marked his words.

What he liked about our relationship, he told me, was that we never spoke about anyone else, not even about people we both knew. We would talk, he used to say, like travelers meeting on a railway platform . . . How I miss him. I liked holding him by the hand, and his holding me with his mind. I liked doing as he said. The clumsi-ness of his blindness did not bother me at all. I admired the fact that he'd been able to survive his own passion for literature. I liked to take the ele-vator to his apartment; and I liked to drive him around, to cut his meat, to try and make our two or three hours together happy ones; I liked to make him tea, to smuggle him a whisky, to listen to music with him; and most of all I liked to listen to him. It always pained me to leave him standing at the door, his eyes turned to follow me, looking lost. Each time, despite our firm arrangement to meet again shortly, I felt that we were not going to see each other again; that he would get fed up with "naughty Lili"—that was what he called me—and with my prattle. I was afraid that something would happen to one of us. And of course, the last time I saw him—at the door for the last time, waiting with me for the elevator for the last time—I was more reassured. I thought that he clung to me a little; I did not think that soon he would have to cling so hard to life.

I remember those strange dinners we shared—sometimes gourmet meals, sometimes not—in discreet restaurants in the 14th arrondissement.

"You know, I was read your 'love letter' just once," he told me right at the beginning. "I liked it very much. But how could I possibly have asked to have it read again so that I could savor your compliments. It would have made me seem self-obsessed." So I made him a tape of it—it took me six hours, I stammered so much—and I put a Band-Aid on the cassette so that he would be able to recognize it by touch. He said afterwards that he sometimes listened to it, in the evenings, when he was depressed and all alone—but no doubt he just wanted to please me. He also used to say: "You've started cutting my steak into pieces that are much too big. Does this mean you're losing your respect for me?" And when I busied myself cutting his food smaller, he would start laughing. "You're a very kind person, aren't you? That's a good sign. Intelligent people are always kind. I only knew one chap who was intelligent and mean-spirited, but he was a homosexual and his life was a desert."

He was also tired of men, of superannuated young men and the prematurely aged boys who

looked to him as a father. He enjoyed—had always enjoyed—only the company of women. "Ah,
but they tire me!" he would say. "Hiroshima is my
fault, Stalin is my fault, their pretentions are my
fault, and their silliness . . ." And he would laugh
at all the intellectual antics of these unnatural or-
phans who wanted him for their father. Sartre a
father? What a ridiculous idea! Sartre a husband?
Just as unthinkable! A lover perhaps. The ease and
warmth of manner which, even blind and half-
paralyzed, he showed toward women were tell-
ing. "You know, when I lost my eyesight and I realized I would not be able to write any more (I was
writing for about ten hours a day for fifty years,
and they were the best moments of my life), when
I realized all that was over for me, it affected me
very deeply and I even thought of killing myself."

I said nothing, but he sensed the terror I felt
at the idea of his martyrdom and added, "But then
I didn't even try. You see, all my life I have been
very happy; I had been, and I was right up until
then, the kind of man, the kind of person, who is
meant to be happy. I couldn't suddenly change. I
continued to be happy out of habit." That was all
he said, but I understood the words he had not
spoken: "So as not to desolate or devastate those
close to me." Especially those women who would
sometimes telephone him at midnight when we

came back from dinner, or in the afternoon while we were having tea. They seemed so demanding, so possessive, so dependent on this infirm blind man who was now deprived of his profession as a writer. These women, by the very excessiveness of their demands on him, restored him to life, the life he had lived till then, as a ladies' man, womanizer and sometimes tenderhearted, sometimes comic storyteller.

He went away on holiday, during that last year; three months' holiday which he shared with three women, an undertaking he met with unfailing kindness and complete fatalism. All summer I thought I had lost him a little. Then he came back and we saw each other again. And then I thought that now I was "for always"; my car was for always, his elevator, tea together, the cassettes, his voice, amused, sometimes tender, always firm. But alas, another kind of "for always" was already there waiting for him alone.

I went to his funeral, not believing it was really happening. Yet it was a splendid funeral, with thousands of people from all walks of life who also loved him and respected him, and accompanied him for miles to his final resting place. These people had not suffered the misfortune of having known him and seen him for a whole year. They did not have dozens of heartrending memories of him. They would not miss him every ten days, every day. And I envied them even while I pitied them.

Since then I have naturally been angered by the shameful stories of Sartre's being senile told by people who were close to him, and I have given up reading certain kinds of reminiscences about him. But I have not forgotten his voice, his laugh, his intelligence, his courage and his goodness. I do not think I will ever really get over his death. For what is one to do sometimes, or to think? He was the only person who could tell me, the only person I could trust, and he has been struck down. Sartre was born on June 21, 1905; I was born on June 21, 1935, but I do not think—nor is it my wish—that I will spend another thirty years on this planet without him.

Reading

In the hierarchy of memory, love of literature ranks far above love itself—human love. For which of us can necessarily remember where or when we met our special "other," and what effect "he" had on us that day? Aren't we in fact more likely to become exhilarated at the thought that on that particular evening we didn't realize all at once that the other person was indeed "him"? Literature, on the other hand, offers up to memory thunderbolts that are far more shattering, final and precise. I know very well where I read, where I discovered the great books in my life; and the external landscapes of my life at the time are there, inextricably linked with my internal landscapes, which for the most part are those of adolescence.

I confess that in the literary domain I covered the most traditional ground imaginable for a French teenager: at thirteen Gide's *The Fruits of the Earth,* at fourteen Camus' *The Rebel,* at sixteen, Rimbaud's *Illuminations.* I took flight across the same landscape over which adolescent souls had been gliding for years and years, which is why I mention these books first: because they were, more than anything else—and much more than a discovery of an author—a discovery of myself, myself as reader, yes, but most of all myself as a living being. In these books I sought an ethic that might appeal to my sense of ethics, a line of thought that would anticipate my own. Certain books, read at the right age, can bring us to precisely this raging state of mingled veneration and self-preoccupation.

It was only later, much later, that I gave up this noble, melodramatic role I thought was mine, that of privileged reader, and it was only later that I discovered literature and its true heroes: writers. In other words, it was only much later that I became more interested in the fate of Julien Sorel than in my own. Just as it was a long time, in my emotional relationships, before I sought in the eyes of the other person his true nature, and not a prettified reflection of myself.

The Fruits of the Earth was the first of these bibles manifestly written especially for me, almost *by me*, the first book which suggested to me what I was, deep down, and what I wanted to be—what it lay within my power to be. Gide is a writer, a spiritual godfather with whom people nowadays are reluctant to claim kinship, and it is perhaps inviting a certain degree of ridicule to cite *Fruits of the Earth* as one's first prayerbook. And still I know exactly how the carob trees smelled when I discovered the first lines, the first orders delivered to Nathanaël. We were living in Dauphiné at the time. It had been raining a great deal that summer and I had been extremely bored, experiencing a rather lyrical state of boredom familiar only to children behind windows streaming with rain in a house in the country. It was on the first day of fine weather after the continuous downpour that I set out, along a path bordered by carob trees, with a book under my arm.

At that time there was a huge poplar in this bit of countryside (of course I went back once, and naturally the poplar had been cut down and in its place was a housing development, and I of course was heartbroken, this being the pattern of our

age). Nevertheless, it was in the shade of this poplar that, thanks to Gide, I discovered that life was
open to me in all its fullness and all its ex-
tremes—something, of course, I might well have
suspected from birth. I was overjoyed at the discovery. Thousands of bright green poplar leaves,
small and densely clustered, trembled high, high
over my head, and each one seemed to me a further joy to come, a joy now expressly promised
by the grace of literature. Before I would ever get
to the top of the tree and reap its last urgent moments of pleasure, I had all those thousands upon
thousands of leaves to pluck, one after the other,
counting off, as it were, the days of my life. As I
couldn't imagine ever growing old, even less ma-
turing, these were so many romantic childish
pleasures massed above me: horses, faces, cars,
glory, books, admiring glances, the sea, boats,
kisses, airplanes in the night—I don't know—
everything that the uncouth and sentimental
imagination of a thirteen-year-old adolescent might
come up with on the spur of the moment. I happened to reread Gide a year or two ago, and while
I felt as if I could see the poplar and smell that
fragrance of carob trees again, all that I thought,
and this almost distractedly, was that it was actually very well written. Thunderbolts too may miss
the mark occasionally.

Immediately after Gide came Camus and *The Rebel*. Recently—in fact only a month or two earlier—I had lost my faith in God, and I was rather stupidly and fearfully proud of the fact. I had lost my faith at Lourdes, where I had by chance been taken and had, by chance, attended a morning benediction. Seeing near me a girl my own age sobbing on a cot from which it looked as if she would never rise, I experienced a feeling of revulsion for the almighty God who could allow such things to be, and in a great rush of indignation and anger I nobly cast Him out of my life, half of which had been spent in boarding schools run by nuns. This metaphysical crisis caused me a loss of appetite at lunchtime and at night brought somber thoughts to my hotel room: the prospect of an earth without God, a world without justice, without pity, without grace, the world in which I would henceforth have to live (a world whose horror I have yet to appreciate fully despite the evidence unremittingly presented me). For two months, like a convalescent, I suffered the irreversible abandonment of an all-powerful God, the extinction, most of all, of a "because" to all possible questions. So I was greatly comforted to discover *The Rebel* and in it the reassuring voice of Camus, also lamenting this burden of absence. God had failed us but there was Man, this gentle dreamer told me; the one replaced the other. The one was the answer to all the questions raised by the negligence of the other.

It was February, I believe; this took place in the mountains. Once again I had been expelled from geography class, repeating the ritual that had been going on for the past three months in the boarding school I was attending. I had taken my skis to climb the slopes—at that time untrammelled by cablecar lines, chair lifts, pizzerias (once again a doleful plaint for our times)—the slopes of Villars-de-Lans. I was sitting on top of my parka, in shirt-sleeves because it was very hot despite the puffs of wind that sent the snow skidding around me like powder, chasing it to the bottom of the valley and the pine trees on the lower slopes, where it piled up in drifts and where I knew I would no doubt land, head first, half an hour later. But I felt good; my arms and legs and back were tired from skiing, I breathed deeply and I could feel the sun drying my hair and skin. I felt I was mistress of my body, my skiis, of my life, mistress of the world; marvelously alone beneath a startlingly blue sky; and it was all one to me that the sky might be empty. Human beings—their spirit, their contradictions, their warmth, their heart, their nerves, their anguish, their desires, their weaknesses, their will, their passions—all awaited me a little way down, a little further on, and, since I was only fourteen, in a little while; and before biting into this world and taking my first steps in it, I still needed two or three years, two wonderful years with nothing to do but pretend to study, and read, understand, work things out and await a wonderful future. What more could God possibly have done for me? I scornfully wondered.

And what's more, what harm could He do me, since I was here with beating heart, warm-blooded living body, and this slope would spread out white and smooth beneath my feet if I only straightened my ankles and pushed myself off? And even if I fell over on the way, there would be men from hot climes, warm-hearted men, in any event, friends, human beings such as this Camus seemed to be, a just protector with faith in Man and his nature, who could see a sense to our existence and was there to remind me of it if I chanced to forget it. It was not so much human beings I believed in at that particular moment, I must admit to myself, but in a man called Camus who wrote well, and whose face on the cover photograph looked attractive and male. Perhaps the non-existence of God might have disturbed me more if Camus had been bald. But no: I have reread *The Rebel* since, and felt that in this case the thunderbolt had found its mark. For it is true that Camus wrote well and that he seemed to have a genuine trust in human nature.

The third of "my books" was the most remote and at the same time the closest to my heart. The most remote because I found in it no nourishment for my narcissistic longings, no directives, no exhortations, not even a model to follow. It was also the closest because in it I discovered the absolute power of words and the way they can be used. Like all French schoolchildren, the only Rimbaud I had read until then were "Le Dormeur du Val" ("The Sleeper in the Valley") and the first verses of *The Drunken Boat.* But that morning, having slept little or not at all during the night because I had been reading—this was the rather early start of the long cycle of my sleepless nights—that morning I lurched wearily out of bed, in the house in Hendaye that my parents had rented for the holidays. I went down to a beach deserted at eight o'clock in the morning, a beach still gray beneath the Basque clouds that scudded low over the sea in tight formation like a fleet of bombers. And I must have settled down beneath "our" bathing tent, with a sweater over my swimsuit, the weather that morning not being July weather. I don't know why I had taken the Rimbaud with me; probably I had a picture of myself along the lines of "Young girl goes to read poetry at dawn on the beach," a vision in keeping with my fantasy of myself (and how much such fantasies could sway the acts and beliefs of a fifteen-year-old in those days—that un-

happy, boastful creature, so repeatedly humili-
ated, and so ridiculously proud; this must still be
so today, no matter what people tell me).

And so, lying flat on my stomach on a beach
towel with my head under the tent and my legs
folded on the cold sand, I opened at random this
white book with thick pages entitled *Illuminations*. I was instantly thunderstruck.

I embraced the summer dawn.

*Nothing yet stirred on the face of the pal-
aces. The water was dead. The shadows still
camped in the woodland road. I walked,
waking quick warm breaths; and gems looked
on, and wings rose without a sound.*

Ah! All at once it was of no consequence
whether God existed, or men were human beings,
or anyone might one day love me. The words
leaped off the page and beat with the wind against
my canvas roof; they rained down upon my head,
image upon image, splendor upon fury.

*Above the road near a laurel wood, I wrapped
her up in her gathered veils, and I felt a little
her immense body. Dawn and the child fell
down at the edge of the wood.*

Waking, it was noon.

Someone had written this, someone had had the genius to write it, the joy of writing it; it was beauty incarnate, definitive proof, all the evidence I ever needed of what I had suspected since I'd read my first unillustrated book—that literature was everything. It was sufficient unto itself; and if others had blindly strayed into business, or into one of the other arts, and didn't know it yet, well at least I now knew. Literature was everything: the best and the worst, fatality; and once you knew this there was no alternative but to grapple with it, with words, literature's slaves, our masters. You had to run with it, strain to leap up to it no matter how high it was. I felt this even after having read what I'd just finished reading, which I would never be able to write myself, but which impelled me by its very beauty to run in the same direction.

In any event, what place was there for hierarchies? When a house is in flames, it's not just the most agile and the fastest who are needed to put out the blaze. When there's a fire, all hands carry water. As if it mattered that the poet Rimbaud had galloped past right at the start . . . Since reading *Illuminations* I have always thought of literature in terms of there being a fire somewhere, everywhere, which I had to put out. And no doubt that's why I've never been able to muster total contempt for even the most calculating, me-

diocre, cynical, vulgar, stupid and glib writers, living or dead. I know that they too heard the alarm
sound one day, and that from time to time they
cannot help but run in desperate haste toward the
fire; and as they stagger around it they burn
themselves just as badly as those who hurl themselves into it. In short, that morning I discovered
what it was I loved, and would continue to love
above all else, for the rest of my life.

After these three discoveries—if I didn't have a
sense of the ridiculous I might call them the discovery of the ethical, of the metaphysical and of
the aesthetic—came my discovery of writers . . .
I gave up my terribly intense dialogues with myself, with my adolescence, and entered the mag-
ical, densely populated and lonesome world of
literary creation. It is always frightfully hot in the
southwest in summer, and in the old family house
where my grandmother lived, the attic, with its
skylights and crumbling beams beneath scorch-
ing-hot tiles, was a real oven, and no one ever went
up there. The "book cupboard"—no French bourgeois home is without one—had long been ban-
ished there. It was there you could find any pro-
scribed book, the most disreputable of which was,
I think, *Les Civilisés,* by Claude Farrère, in that
good old yellow-bound edition with dark engrav-

ings that is remembered fondly only by those of my generation and older. Otherwise it was a bewildering jumble of Delly, Pierre Loti, La Fontaine, the Masque series, as well as—miraculously—three Dostoevsky novels and a volume of Montaigne's essays, and, sole survivor of the fourteen he had written, one volume by Proust, *Albertine Disparue (The Fugitive)*. I won't dwell at length upon the attic's charms; it had the smell, the dust and the allure of every attic in everyone's childhood—everyone, at least, lucky enough to have had an attic in his childhood. I clearly remember sweating profusely without moving a muscle as I sat in an old armchair with worn velvet covers, surprised occasionally to hear the footsteps of someone foolhardy enough to venture out for a stroll round town at siesta time.

I've come across many people since who haven't been able to read Proust because they "couldn't manage it," because Swann, the celebrated *Swann's Way* they were always presented with, confounded and bored them. And I think that had I too begun with Odette's affairs and the narrator's childhood, I would have found it much more difficult to penetrate these two interminable worlds. With *Albertine Disparue* I entered into the drama at once, I began with the only vagary of fortune in the whole of Proust's oeuvre, the only event, the only accident, the only instance when

172

Proust allows chance to speak, and where chance takes the form of a telegram: "My poor friend, our little Albertine is no more. Forgive me for breaking this terrible news to you who were so fond of her. She was thrown by her horse against a tree while she was out riding." I began at this line and plunged like a stone into the depths of sorrow, into a despair teased to madness, relentlessly scrutinized, expounded upon, and lashed by the Narrator.

It was along this path that I led many friends to love Proust, friends who had been put off by Swann. Like me, they were at once gripped by *Albertine Disparue*. But I discovered something else in this book that I have never ceased to reread, along with the other volumes, of course; I discovered that there was no limit, no point beyond which you could not go, that truth—human truth, that is—was everywhere, and everywhere open to investigation, that it was both unattainable and the only object of desire.

I discovered that the subject matter of any work, from the moment the work concerned itself with human beings, was boundless; that if I wished one day—and were able—to describe the birth and death of any feeling whatsoever, I could spend my whole life doing it, write millions of pages on the subject and never complete the task, never reach the end of it, never be able to say, "That's it. I've done it." I discovered that one would never—that I would never—get beyond halfway, beyond a fraction of the way toward achieving my goal. I discovered that the human being who replaced God—or maybe didn't, who was trustworthy or good for nothing, this handful of dust whose consciousness was all-embracing—was the only prey I was interested in, the only quarry I would never manage to bring down but would sometimes, perhaps, fleetingly grasp, in one of those great moments of happiness which the act of writing bestows. I also discovered in Proust, besides the glorious madness of writing, this passion that cannot be controlled and is always kept under control, the truth that writing was no idle occupation, that it was not easy, that, contrary to an idea already current at the time, there were no more true writers than there were true painters and true musicians. I discovered that a talent for writing was a gift of fate bestowed on very few people, that the poor fools whose intention was to make a career or a hobby of it were nothing more than wretched desecrators. Writing requires a precise, precious and rare talent—the truth of this is unseemly and almost incongruous these days. In any event, literature, with its gentle disdain for its false priests and pretenders, takes its own revenge, turning those who dare meddle with it, even at arm's length, into impotent and bitter cripples—and gives them nothing, except sometimes, with cruel intent, a transient success that will torment them for life.

And so I learned too from Proust how difficult and important were the scales of merit in the realm that was my passion. In fact, I learned everything through Proust.

But there is today one thing that I must confess, as I think back to the first time I read these books and to the landscapes they evoke: that if I am today unable to explain, or even understand, the progress of my life; if I know nothing, have learned nothing in the course of a life that could readily be described as turbulent, nonetheless these four books, of which I now value no more than half, have always been there, serving me as springboards or compasses. For years my soul has taken its bearings from them; it is to them that my most vivid, fullest memories are attached. It was not just my mind, but my sense of smell, hearing, sight and even touch that were marked in those instants; while the heart's memories have left nothing but complete fuzziness or else, as if by contrast, satiety of one sense only. The brilliance of an eye close against one's own, of first love, the smell of coffee and rain during one's first breakup are heightened in the extreme, but at the cost of everything else. Was it raining during that first kiss? Did he say goodbye with downcast eyes? I don't know, I was living too intensely. And it was only when I let others live in my place, when I read about them, that my own existence became at last wholly accessible to me.